The Shocking Discovery

Connie Griffith and her family live in Boone, North Carolina. She and her husband serve at the headquarters of Africa Evangelical Fellowship. This is her first series of American children's novels.

The Tootie McCarthy Series

BOOK 5

The Shocking Discovery

Connie Griffith

BakerBooks

A Division of Baker Book House Co
Grand Rapids, Michigan 49516

© 1994 by Connie Griffith

Cover illustration by Jim Hsieh, © 1994 Baker Book House

Published by Baker Books
a division of Baker Book House Company
P.O. Box 6287, Grand Rapids, MI 49516-6287

Printed in the United States of America

Library of Congress Cataloging-in-Publication Data

Griffith, Connie
    The shocking discovery / Connie Griffith.
        p.   cm.—(The Tootie McCarthy series ; bk. 5)
    Sequel to: Mysterious rescuer.
    Summary: In 1928 fourteen-year-old Tootie McCarthy tries to follow her mother's example of faith as she deals with the taunts of a local rich girl, accusations about a bank robbery, and a devastating tornado, while helping take care of her retarded younger brother on the family farm near Siren, Wisconsin.
    ISBN 0-8010-3866-9
    [1. Country life—Fiction. 2. Irish Americans—Fiction. 3. Christian life—Fiction. 4. Mentally handicapped—Fiction. 5. Tornadoes—Fiction.] I. Title. II. Series: Griffith, Connie. Tootie McCarthy series; bk. 5.
PZ7.G88175Sh   1994
[Fic]—dc20   93-8422

Scripture quotations are from the King James Version of the Bible.

To
my twin, Bonnie Kopp,
who helps me continue to discover

Tootie bit down on her stubby thumbnail. She couldn't tell whether her ninth grade teacher, Mr. Brightenger, was trying to scare the class, or if he was simply giving information. She scooted to the edge of her chair and firmly planted her scuffed brown shoes under her desk.

"Twisters!" Mr. Brightenger repeated. "They destroy property and take lives every year. This is the season for twisters, or tornadoes as some prefer to call them. All of us here in Siren must be prepared."

Sylvia Shinler shot her hand up in the air.

Mr. Brightenger looked her way. "Yes, Miss Shinler, do you have something to add?"

"My dad has our cellar full of food. We have enough food down there to feed everyone in the whole state of Wisconsin!"

Tootie hated the way Sylvia always drew attention to the fact that she was from the richest family in town. *So her dad owns the Mercantile! Why does she always have to brag?*

"It's good to hear that people are prepared," their teacher said. Then he went into a spasm of coughing. "Excuse me, I still have this terrible cough." Finally he turned back to Sylvia. "Your father also needs to store plenty of water in that cellar of his. Good, clean water! Now, let's go over what causes a twister to form."

Tootie tried to concentrate on Mr. Brightenger's explanation about how cold air sinks while warm, moist air rises, and how the inrushing air begins to rotate. But it all seemed confusing to her. *Besides, what's the chance of something like that happening here?* she thought.

As she sat staring at her teacher, other things began to fill her mind—like the way her fifteen-year-old sister, Pearl, had quit school. Since the bus accident for which Pearl was partly to blame, her sister had refused to return to school. And that was more than two and a half months ago. Then Tootie thought about how depressed her father was. Since they had moved from the city to the farm, he moped around. He wasn't at all like his usual happy self; he hardly ever joked anymore.

Suddenly a third thought crossed Tootie's mind and her thin lips spread into a smile. She couldn't help it. Just thinking about the way her little retarded brother, Buddy, had adjusted to life on the farm made her happy. Buddy had not only learned to do jobs like stacking wood, but he had also learned to chop it. Tootie almost giggled as she thought of the huge pile of chopped wood that almost reached to the roof of their barn!

Mr. Brightenger's cough brought Tootie back to the subject at hand. "Twisters do curious things. They can drive a piece of straw into a tree or turn automobiles over and over. Often they carry people and animals for hundreds of feet. I've even heard they sometimes strip the feathers from chickens."

Tootie giggled.

"What's funny, Miss McCarthy?" Mr. Brightenger asked.

Tootie answered before thinking. "Oh, I was just imagining how odd a naked chicken would look."

Sylvia Shinler leaned from her chair and glared in Tootie's face. She said half under her breath, "Everything's funny to you! Well, someday something is going to wipe that smile right off your face."

"That's enough!" Mr. Brightenger demanded of Sylvia. "You and Miss McCarthy can settle your differences outside of class. But for now, let's continue our lesson on twisters."

Sylvia plopped down in her chair.

Just then the bell rang. The students stood at attention beside their desks until Mr. Brightenger dismissed them. Arl Neilson hurried over to Tootie. "I'll meet you at the bus," he whispered.

"Who do you think's driving today?" Tootie asked. Since the school bus accident, teachers had taken turns driving the replacement bus. A brand new 1928 vehicle had been borrowed from the nearby town of Webster until Siren could purchase its own. The teachers appreciated being loaned a new bus, but having to drive the students to and from school didn't make them happy.

Arl was about to answer Tootie's question when Mr. Brightenger began ordering all the boys to file out of the school through one door and the girls through another. Tootie thought it was a stupid rule; they had never filed out like that when she lived in the city. She grabbed her books and the syrup pail she used as a lunch bucket. She quickly put on her old brown coat and red scarf, and then hurried toward the door.

Sylvia Shinler nudged Tootie in the back as they were going down the steps in front of the school. Tootie stumbled and almost lost her balance.

"Is now a good time to settle our differences?" Sylvia asked with a sneer.

Tootie took a deep breath and held it. She began counting to ten, trying desperately to control her temper.

But before she got to three, Sylvia continued, "By the way, no one's seen hide nor hair of your sister since the bus accident. I bet Pearl's just too embarrassed to show her face after what she did!"

"I'd be quiet if I were you!" Tootie warned. She had already determined that under no circumstance would she fight with Sylvia. She'd fought with her before, and it always turned out awful. In fact, lately, Tootie had asked God for help in controlling her temper and had even begun praying for Sylvia.

But Sylvia wouldn't back down. She shook her thick black curls, pulled up the collar of her purple coat against the spring breeze, and took one step closer to Tootie.

"Your sister just couldn't leave our bus driver alone.

Oh, no! Pearl had to go and kiss Carly Frank. We all saw it! And then he lost control of the bus. No one even knows where Carly Frank is. He's run away! And now our town has to buy another bus and it's all your sister's fault! You McCarthys should pack up and go back to the city! We've had nothing but trouble since you arrived."

"You haven't seen trouble!" Tootie said, momentarily forgetting her prayers. "Why don't you forget about that stupid accident? It happened months ago. Just forget it!"

"Holey moley!" Sylvia cried as Mr. Brightenger passed. "Did you hear the way Tootie talks to me?"

"Hurry along!" their teacher demanded. He motioned Tootie and Sylvia toward the bus. "Get on that bus if you want a ride home!"

The moment their teacher walked away, Sylvia smirked at her girlfriends and then back at Tootie. Tootie thought the way Sylvia's cheeks puffed out looked ridiculous, almost like two rose-colored balloons. It was all she could do not to make a face back at her enemy.

"You're getting off easy this time," Sylvia said half under her breath. "Just wait. Your time is coming!"

"So is yours!" Tootie responded, and tried to stretch an inch or two taller. Then she turned and marched toward the bus, her short reddish-brown curls bouncing as they escaped around her scarf.

"Don't let Sylvia get to you," Arl said as Tootie slipped

next to him in the rear seat of the bus. "It's obvious she's pushing for a fight."

"She makes me so mad!" Tootie said.

Lavern Roy turned around and leaned over the back of the seat. "Hey, Arl, don't stop her. Tootie's just the one to give it to Sylvia!" He shoved his stringy hair out of his eyes.

"I'm through with fighting," Tootie confided in her most grown-up voice.

Lavern Roy looked at his two brothers and then at Arl. They all burst out laughing.

Lavern's brothers, Lawrence and Leo, were crowded onto the seat next to him. Lavern was fifteen, the same age as Pearl. Lawrence was almost fourteen, just like Tootie, and Leo was the youngest. They lived in a farmhouse about a half mile down the road from the old place Tootie's parents had bought. During the past months since moving to Siren, Tootie had become friends with all three of them and with Arl Neilson, who helped his father on a nearby farm.

"By the way," Lavern said, "tell that pretty sister of yours that we hope she gets better. We miss her!"

Leo shoved his brother almost off the seat. "*You* miss her," he teased.

Tootie smiled. It was time to be honest with her friends. "Pearl's not sick," she said quietly. "I think you already know that. Really, it's just like Sylvia said— Pearl's embarrassed about how she caused that bus accident."

Lawrence spoke up. "After the way you and Buddy

helped with the rescue, you'd think that would make up for it."

"You'd think so," Tootie agreed. "Anyway, Pearl can't get over the fact that Carly Frank skipped town. She thought . . . well, she thought that he liked her or something." She hated talking about things like this.

The students were still filing onto the bus, and Sylvia had already settled herself in a seat toward the middle. But she'd been watching Tootie. Suddenly she blurted out, "Hey, look at Tootie. She's just as boy crazy as her sister! Those Irish girls flirt with anybody who wears pants! Watch. Tootie's about to kiss the Roy boys and Arl Neilson!"

Several of Sylvia's friends snickered.

This was too much! Tootie jumped to her feet. She couldn't let Sylvia get away with this!

But Tootie wasn't the only one who had jumped up. Arl and all three of the Roys were standing, ready to make Sylvia take back every word.

Just then Mr. Brightenger got onto the bus. "I'm your driver today," he announced. "Sit down, everyone!" He stared hard at the group in the back of the bus.

Tootie yanked off her scarf and stuffed it into her pocket. She clenched her fists and slowly sat back down.

Mr. Brightenger went on to say that he wanted complete silence while he drove the bus and that everyone was to get out some homework and begin studying. "I'm not used to driving such a large vehicle," he explained. "At least the winter is over, and this bus has wheels and not runners like the old one. Anyway, for your own safety, keep silent while I drive."

Tootie didn't give Sylvia the satisfaction of looking her way. She also felt too embarrassed to look at the Roy boys or Arl. Quickly she got out her notes on twisters and stared down at the nearly blank page.

It wasn't long before Mr. Brightenger turned off U.S. Route 35 and headed down Main Street. They passed the bank and the church on the right and the butcher shop and post office on the left. Several students got off at the corner, and the bus proceeded to the next block past Dr. Treadwell's and the bakery, which was no longer in business. Tootie stared at the abandoned building. It reminded her of the bakery in the city her parents had sold to buy the farm and move here to the country. *If only we could own that bakery,* Tootie thought. *That would solve a lot of our problems.*

Her thoughts were interrupted when Mr. Brightenger stopped the bus in front of the Mercantile. Sylvia lived in back of the big, brown Shinler Mercantile Store with the Siren Town Hall above.

Just then Sylvia's father came out of the store with an extremely large woman, followed by a man who appeared about twenty. They hurried over toward the bus.

"Who's that?" Tootie whispered.

"Never seen them before," Arl said. "Hey, Lawrence, who are the newcomers?"

Lawrence shrugged.

Everyone watched as Mr. Shinler introduced the newcomers to their school teacher. "This is Mrs. Deuce, our new postmistress. She's a real government official."

Their teacher got to his feet and shook hands with the woman.

"And this is Julius, her son," Mr. Shinler continued the introductions.

Their teacher and Julius shook hands.

Mr. Shinler jabbed his thumb toward Julius. "There's talk about hiring this young man as the school custodian and bus driver. Town council meets tonight."

"You can have this job," Mr. Brightenger grumbled. "The sooner, the better."

Julius turned and waved at the busload of students. Tootie noticed he was missing the pointer finger on his left hand.

Just then Sylvia said loud enough for everyone to hear, "He'd better be warned about Pearl McCarthy before she kisses him and makes us have another bus wreck!"

Suddenly Mrs. Deuce pushed past her son and maneuvered her large frame into the center aisle. "Don't be disturbed by that remark, young lady." Mrs. Deuce stared directly at Tootie. "Yes, you—the one with the red scarf stuffed into your pocket. I predict you will get even in the near future."

Mrs. Deuce roared with laughter at the shocked expression on Tootie's face. She clapped her hands several times and then began to rub them vigorously as she spoke to everybody on the bus. "I'm not only the new Siren postmistress; I can also tell your futures. Me and my son bought us a place outside of town, and you're all welcome. So are your parents. I'll read your palms anytime—or tea leaves for that matter. It's a hobby of mine—mighty interesting!" With that the large woman laughed again, turned, and lumbered out of the bus.

No one said a word. Even Sylvia Shinler was shocked into silence.

The bus pulled away from Shinler Mercantile and proceeded across the railroad tracks and out toward the farmland where most of the students lived. Tootie kept her nose buried in her books as she went over and over what Mrs. Deuce had said.

Mr. Brightenger drove carefully, stopping to let students off at the right places. Finally he came to the stop for Tootie, Arl, and the Roy boys.

Tootie quickly grabbed her stuff. She hurried up the aisle and off the bus before anyone could say a word about Mrs. Deuce speaking directly to her. The whole incident gave Tootie the creeps.

She was hurrying down the lane to her house when Arl and the Roy boys caught up with her.

"Wait!" Arl hollered. "What was all that about? How do you think Mrs. Deuce knew your scarf was in your pocket? She couldn't have seen it."

"Is she a witch?" the youngest Roy asked.

"No," Lavern and Lawrence said at the same time. Then Lawrence added, "At least I don't think she's a witch."

"Don't be silly!" Tootie said and slowed her pace. "She's a postmistress—a government official for pity's sake! How could someone like that be a witch? There must be some simple explanation for how she knew about my scarf. She must've seen me stuff it into my pocket. That's all!"

"But she says she can tell the future," Lavern reminded Tootie. "And she predicted that someday you'll get even with Sylvia. Don't you want that?"

Tootie stopped and looked at her friends. "No, I don't. Well, not if it has anything to do with Mrs. Deuce. That woman gives me the creeps!"

"Me, too," Arl said. "I've got to hurry and go do chores." He waved as he went toward the Olsons' farm, which sat slightly back off the road to the right. Arl and his dad did most of the work around the place. Arl stopped and called over his shoulder, "I'm getting up early tomorrow and going fishing before school. Want to come?"

"No," Tootie said.

"How about Buddy? Think he'd like to come? Olof's usually with me." The Olsons' simple son and Buddy were becoming friends. One of the reasons Tootie's parents had moved to the country was because of Buddy's condition. And, surprisingly, it was Buddy who had adjusted to farm life quickest. He had found a friend in Olof, a boy very similar to himself.

"The only thing Buddy would catch that early in the morning is a cold," Tootie said and smiled.

"Hey, Arl, I'll go with you," Lawrence said. Then Lavern and Leo decided to join them.

Tootie walked on ahead as they made their plans. There would be plenty of chores for her to do at home.

The moment Tootie walked into the farmyard, she knew something was terribly wrong. Father was storming out of the house, heading for the barn, with a rolled newspaper in his grasp. As always, he wore his dark pin-striped suit and derby hat. He owned absolutely no work clothes, and he refused to buy any. Donald McCarthy hadn't noticed his daughter's approach. He kept mumbling angrily to himself as he slapped the paper across the palm of his hand.

For a moment Tootie leaned against the tamarack tree at the edge of their yard until her father entered the barn. She'd never seen him so distraught.

She waited for the Roys to pass and head for their place before she went into her family's square, unpainted farmhouse. The only door to the house led directly into the kitchen. Mother was stoking the fire in the big black stove. She looked up as Tootie entered.

"Did you have a good day?" Eve McCarthy asked in her gentle manner and quickly wiped away a tear.

Tootie nodded and removed her coat, throwing it over one of the ladder-back chairs.

"Sit down and have a glass of milk." Not waiting for a reply, Eve picked up a bucket and poured Tootie a tall glass of the creamy liquid. "Buddy did the milking about a half hour ago."

"Isn't it wonderful?" Tootie said, trying to lighten the mood. "Buddy just loves the farm!"

"I know. It makes moving here all worthwhile." Eve

quickly pressed back the few strands of graying hair which had escaped from the bun at the back of her head. Then she turned toward the counter and began shredding a head of cabbage. "There's nothing too big for God, Tootie," Mother said. "We can always count on him. Never forget that, lass."

"What's the matter?" Tootie asked anxiously.

"Nothing to worry your pretty little head about," Eve replied. "Hurry along and help Buddy fill this wood box." Mother shoved her foot against the empty crate next to the stove.

It was obvious Mother was deeply troubled. But Tootie knew her mother would never confide in her about any of their problems. Tootie hurried into the bedroom she shared with Pearl and Buddy.

Pearl was standing by the dresser, brushing her shiny black hair. It was parted straight down the middle. Pearl put down the brush and began twisting and tucking the hair on one side into a neat bun close to her ear. After pinning it in place, she began on the other side.

Tootie started to change into an old pair of trousers and a faded flannel shirt.

"I didn't expect you home so soon," Pearl said, still staring at her reflection. Then she dabbed on some pink lipstick.

"I come home at the same time every day," Tootie replied. "And so did you when you went to school." Tootie flopped down on the double bed which she shared with her sister. "Come on, Pearl, everyone's asking for you. We want you to come back."

Pearl turned, put her hands on her slim hips, and glared at Tootie. "I'll never go back to that school as long as I live! I'm fifteen, and that's old enough to quit! Besides, I'm making plans of my own."

"What do you mean?" Tootie jumped to her feet. "What plans?"

"You'll see." Pearl turned and, once again, stared at her reflection. She leaned over the dresser and looked closely at her two false front teeth. "I hate these stupid teeth!"

Tootie sighed in exasperation. She didn't want to stay and listen to Pearl's list of complaints one more time. Besides, if Pearl didn't draw so much attention to her teeth, they would hardly be noticed.

"I've got to go," Tootie said and hurried to the door. "See you at supper."

Tootie grabbed her coat and hurried outside. She almost bumped into Buddy. He wore his coat and an old cap with flaps, which covered his ears. He pushed his cap back slightly, exposing his broad forehead. He smiled and his small eyes almost disappeared into his chubby cheeks. "Toot! Toot! Toot!" he greeted.

"My Buddy Boy!" Tootie responded, planting a kiss on the tip of his nose.

Buddy clapped excitedly, letting his tongue hang out.

It wasn't long before they had filled the wagon with wood and were pulling it to the house to unload. Soon the crate by the stove was overflowing with chunks of wood and all the kindling they might need if the fire burned out during the night.

Then Tootie and Buddy hurried back to the barn to make sure Babe, their big black-and-white holstein, had hay. Father greeted them as they entered the barn, and then went back to fiddling with the engine of the open-bed truck he had borrowed to move the family to the country.

Finally Donald slammed down the hood and wiped his fingers on his clean white handkerchief. "Looks like all is in fine working order. I'll need to be getting this vehicle back to the city real soon."

Tootie stared at her father in surprise. "But I thought the owner of the truck was coming here with one of his friends to get it. Wasn't that the plan?"

"Plans change," Donald said and flicked several of Tootie's reddish-brown curls. Then he began dusting her coat sleeve with his hankie to remove several pieces of hay.

That night at the supper table, over a plate of cabbage and fried onions, Father announced his plans. "I'm going back to the city tomorrow morning. I need to return the truck. Your mother and I've been talking it all over. I'm going to stay in the city and look for a job."

"A . . . a job?" Tootie sputtered. "But you've got a job here—on the farm—with us!"

"I'm no farmer," Donald admitted. "I guess I'm a pencil pusher. I miss my auditing work, and that's the kind of job I'm going to look for."

Tootie knew her father was good with balancing business figures; he'd worked hard at it when they had the bakery. *But why can't he forget all that now,* Tootie thought, *and stay here and work on our farm? Besides, it was his idea in the first place that we move here to the country. He's even spent all my reward money on buying this place!*

"But—" Tootie began.

"No arguing!" Donald held up his hands. "Eve and I have already discussed this matter." Then Father slowly looked around the table. Buddy was slopping up his cabbage in a most noisy manner. It was obvious he hadn't understood one word of the conversation.

Pearl had long since pushed her plate away. She sat perched on the edge of her chair, twisting her cloth napkin round and round. Suddenly she jumped to her feet knocking over her chair. "I'm leaving with you!" Pearl cried. "I'm going crazy in this awful place!"

"But we're a family—you can't leave!" Tootie cried.

Mother got up from the table and placed a gentle hand on Tootie's shoulder. "Don't worry, lass."

Tootie didn't want to listen to the long discussion ahead. Besides, she knew her parents would never allow Pearl to leave. What would she do in the city? And Father probably wouldn't leave either; he just couldn't.

Tootie helped Buddy finish his meal and then she hurried him away from the table.

Later that night after Pearl and their parents finally quit talking, Tootie settled down at the table to do her homework by the light of the kerosene lantern. She believed with all her heart that everything would be all right in the morning.

Before daybreak, Tootie got up to check on Buddy. She lit the kerosene lantern on the bedside table, and a warm glow immediately filled the crowded bedroom.

Buddy had thrashed about during the night, leaving most of his brown wool blanket on the braided, multicolored scatter rug beside the bed. As Tootie picked up the blanket to rearrange it over her sleeping brother, she noticed it was damp. In fact, Buddy's entire bed was wet.

"Wake up, little brother," Tootie said and shook him gently. "Come on, you've wet your bed."

Pearl turned over onto her tummy, pulled the covers over her head, and grumbled, "Keep the chatter down over there! I want to sleep."

"Come on, Buddy," Tootie urged even louder. She wasn't about to keep quiet for Pearl's sake. "Buddy Boy, you'll catch your death of cold if you don't get out of these." She tugged on the sleeve of his favorite soft blue pajamas.

Just then Mother pushed wide their bedroom door. "Thanks for changing him," Eve said as Tootie began to undress her brother. "I thought that might happen with all the emotions last night after supper. I'll stoke the fire and get a bucket of warm water ready for the soiled things."

After Tootie washed and dressed Buddy, she hurried to get herself ready for school. She barely had time to slip into her brown serge dress and go to the outdoor toilet.

Mother had hot porridge ready when Tootie and Buddy went to the kitchen, and the three of them sat down to eat. After Eve thanked God for their night of rest and food, she began spooning the cereal into their bowls.

"What's the matter with Daddy?" Tootie asked. "Why isn't he eating?"

Eve placed a bowl in front of Tootie. "Your father's had a lot on his mind. He didn't sleep well last night, so he decided he'd better get a few more winks this morning."

"I hope he feels better after a good night's sleep," Tootie said. "I hated all that talk last night about leaving."

"Don't you go worrying," Mother said. "I'm sure everything will work out."

Tootie quickly finished her cereal. Then she cut two slices of bread and put them into the syrup pail she used as her lunch bucket. The bucket was beginning to rust, giving her bread-and-butter sandwiches a tinny taste. She wished she could find something else to use as a lunch bucket. Finally Tootie quickly ran a brush through her short curls, said a hurried good-bye to her brother, and grabbed her coat and scarf. Seeing the scarf made her think of Mrs. Deuce.

"Mama," Tootie said, "tonight I want to tell you and Daddy about a new woman in town. She's really strange."

Eve looked up from doing the breakfast dishes with a faraway look in her eyes. "What?"

Tootie could tell her mother wasn't paying attention. The last thing she'd be concerned about was the new postmistress and her hobby of reading palms and tea leaves.

"Nothing, Mama," Tootie responded. "See you tonight."

The Roy boys were waiting for her by the tamarack tree. They were huddled against the morning cold in their old coats. None of them wore hats, and their stringy hair blew around their faces. Tootie could see their breath fogging the air.

"Isn't Pearl coming?" Lavern asked.

"No," Tootie said. Then she added, "But I hope she will soon. She needs to get back into school."

Leo laughed. "That's Lavern's dream. He's in love with your sister."

"Shut up!" Lavern shouted, and started chasing his younger brother down the road to the bus stop. Tootie and Lawrence followed.

"Arl and I each caught a walleyed pike this morning," Lawrence said, swinging his school books by a rough leather strap. "My fish was huge. You should've seen it!"

Tootie laughed. "I bet if I'd gone, mine would've been bigger!"

They both laughed because they knew Tootie had never gone fishing in her life. But she determined that the next time Arl or Lawrence asked her to join them, she'd give it a try.

When Tootie and the Roy boys got to the main road, Arl Neilson was already there. He was standing in front of a large sign which had been nailed to a tree. The sign read: PALM READER. Under the words was a red arrow pointing to a small, run-down house set back off the road.

"Can you believe it?" Arl said as Tootie and the Roys hurried over. "That must be Mrs. Deuce's place."

"She certainly didn't waste any time putting up that sign," Lavern commented. "Quiet, here she comes!"

Mrs. Deuce and her son, Julius, hurried out of the house and began walking toward them. Mrs. Deuce wore a straight wool skirt, which came about an inch or two below her knees. The skirt was too tight for her hips, so it rode up slightly in the front as she walked, exposing the fat around her knees. She had on a matching navy-blue coat, made exactly like a man's jacket.

As Mrs. Deuce approached, she threw back her head and laughed. "What's the matter? Haven't you ever seen a postmistress before?"

"No," Tootie said, "I didn't even know a woman could get such a job." She wanted to add that she'd also never seen a postmistress who read palms.

Just then the school bus came into view. Mr. Brightenger was coughing as he stopped the bus, borrowed from Webster, by the edge of the road. He looked relieved when he saw Julius Deuce. "I heard that the town council hired you last night to be the new bus driver and the school janitor."

"That's right," Julius said without a hint of emotion.

Mr. Brightenger responded, "Well, young man, you can begin right now!" He immediately stood up and pointed to the driver's seat. "It's all yours!"

With a grin Julius took his new place behind the wheel as Tootie and her friends filed into the bus and down the aisle. Mrs. Deuce sat near the front in a seat meant for two. She took out some papers from her purse and began reading.

"Aren't the Deuces an odd lot?" Lavern whispered as he slipped into one of the rear seats.

Tootie nodded, and so did the others. All the way into Siren, they continued guessing how Julius might have lost his finger and how it would feel to have your fortune told. Lavern even suggested that Mrs. Deuce probably had read everyone's mail and that's how she could tell the future.

"I bet you're right," Tootie agreed with a mischievous smile. "Can't you just imagine Mrs. Deuce snooping around everyone's mail?"

Then they stifled their laughter and continued to speak low so Mrs. Deuce couldn't hear.

It wasn't long before Julius stopped the bus in front of Shinler Mercantile and opened the door. Sylvia and several other students came hurrying out of the store.

Just then Mrs. Deuce stood, straightened her wool skirt, turned around, and looked directly at Tootie, Arl, Lavern, Lawrence, and Leo. She smiled, revealing a set of perfectly white teeth. Then she said, "You at the back of the bus, your conversation has been most enlightening."

Sylvia Shinler had just come alongside Mrs. Deuce, and she snickered at the woman's comment. As usual Sylvia wore her purple coat, purple knit hat, and gloves. Tootie thought her classmate looked like a plum. But this morning Sylvia looked even more ridiculous because she'd attempted to apply a purple shade of rouge. She smiled in a coy manner at Mrs. Deuce as though she and the new postmistress were already the best of friends.

"That's Tootie McCarthy back there in the midst of all those boys," Sylvia announced. "You'll soon learn that Tootie's always smack-dab in the center of trouble. If there's anything happening in Siren, you can count on one of the McCarthys being the cause."

Tootie couldn't believe it. How dare Sylvia talk about her like that! She wanted to tear off Sylvia's hat and stuff it in her mouth.

But before Tootie could react, Mrs. Deuce responded, "It sounds to me as though you're also smack-dab in the center of trouble. I'm surprised that nose of yours isn't purple to match the rest of you. You're quite the busybody!" Then the new postmistress turned her large frame and left the bus without a backward glance.

Tootie had never heard anyone talk in such a manner to Sylvia Shinler. Most adults doted on her. It was even more surprising that Mr. Brightenger had ignored the whole thing and looked straight ahead.

Without a word, Sylvia flopped down into the seat which Mrs. Deuce had just vacated, and the bus moved forward.

Tootie forgot the incident as soon as they got to school. She noticed that Mr. Brightenger still coughed in class, but he was in a better mood than he'd been in weeks. The hiring of a bus driver and janitor must have done a lot to lighten his load.

Everyone saw Julius Deuce from time to time throughout the day—sweeping the hallway, cleaning bathrooms, even wiping down blackboards. He was quiet and kept totally to himself. Twenty-year-old Julius did not have the commanding nature of his mother, the postmistress. While she was somebody you'd remember, Julius was soon forgotten after the first look. There was nothing distinguishing about him, except possibly his left hand.

However, on the way home Tootie knew something had gone terribly wrong in Siren. The bus had turned down Main Street, and as they passed the bank they saw a crowd out in front. Tootie felt certain that several men pointed directly at her as the bus passed by. In fact, she thought she heard Mr. Shinler yell, "That's her. That's the McCarthy girl!"

"What's happening?" Arl asked, and slammed shut his math book. "It looks like they're pointing at you."

"What's going on?" one of the Roy boys added.

Sylvia turned and glared toward the back of the bus. "What have you done this time, Tootie?"

Tootie looked from Sylvia to the men outside the bus, her eyes wide.

Men started running after the bus, waving it down. "Stop! Stop!" they hollered.

As the bus came to a stop, several members of the town council clambered on and pushed their way down the aisle toward Tootie. Not one of the students moved. Mr. Shinler was leading the pack, wheezing loudly. "Where's your father?" he demanded.

Tootie didn't answer. She couldn't!

"You heard me!" Mr. Shinler shouted and ran his hands through his thinning hair, making it stand straight on end. "Your father has robbed the bank. I'm broke! Absolutely broke! Every penny I had was in that bank!"

"We're all broke," another man shouted. "Even the bus fund was taken."

"Hold on. We don't have proof that it was Donald McCarthy," a third councilman reminded them.

"He was seen leaving town in that truck of his," Sylvia Shinler's father shouted hotly. "That's proof enough for me!"

Tootie took a deep breath to steady herself. Finally she said, her voice barely more than a whisper, "Leaving? You saw my father leaving town? That's impossible!"

Suddenly the full impact of what the councilmen were saying dawned on Tootie. She jumped to her feet. "My father would never rob a bank!" she shouted. "How dare you accuse him! Besides, my father wouldn't leave town without saying good-bye. Never!" Hot angry tears stung her hazel eyes.

Mr. Shinler glared wildly. "Your father left town, all right. He's robbed us blind!"

Arl stood tall next to Tootie. "Mr. McCarthy wouldn't steal a thing. You're accusing the wrong man."

"That's right," Lawrence added. "Besides, don't you remember how he helped everyone after the accident? A robber wouldn't do that!"

"That's right!" Lavern and Leo agreed.

Odd noises were coming from the middle of the bus. It was Sylvia Shinler, white-faced and whimpering. "What are we going to do?" she cried. "How are we going to live without money?"

"Let's get the sheriff to come over from Webster," one of the councilmen suggested. "He'll find the truth."

"I know the truth!" Mr. Shinler spouted.

"I think we all do," another man agreed. "So let's hurry and make that call." The group turned to leave.

Tootie couldn't believe it. How dare they accuse her father and then march away!

Sylvia began crying hysterically as she followed her father out of the bus. Then she said loud enough for all to hear, "Oh, Daddy, how are you going to buy me that new coat you promised? The McCarthys ruin everything!"

Tootie didn't wait for Sylvia to say another word. She stormed down the aisle. Somehow she had to make Sylvia stop!

Suddenly Tootie heard a familiar call. "Toot! Toot! Toot!"

She stopped on the bottom step of the bus and stared in disbelief at her brother, Buddy. He was right there, almost in front of her, proudly holding the handle of his little red wagon. He smiled broadly, leaned his head to the right, and let his tongue hang out. Eve was coming down the street not far behind him.

Sylvia pushed past Buddy, shoving him hard in the chest. Buddy fell backward into the dirt and began to cry.

In a panic, Tootie ran and knelt by Buddy's side. He wasn't hurt but it was obvious he was scared.

Tootie's mother stepped in front of Sylvia. "What's the meaning of this?" Eve demanded.

Mr. Shinler interrupted, "Where's your husband, Mrs. McCarthy?"

The councilmen moved in closer. Most of the students were hanging out the bus windows.

"My husband's gone," Eve admitted, squaring her shoulders. "Donald and our daughter, Pearl, left this morning. They went back to the city to look for jobs. My son and I have walked into town to buy us a few groceries. What's going on?"

"They're accusing Daddy of robbing the bank!" Tootie shouted in anger while helping Buddy to his feet.

"What?" Eve asked, incredulously.

"No one should be accusing anyone of being a robber," Mrs. Deuce said. She had been standing on the edge of the crowd. The postmistress stepped forward. She was holding a package to her ample chest.

"You know nothing about this matter," Mr. Shinler said with obvious anger.

Mrs. Deuce didn't look offended. Instead, she said, "You're right, I don't. But it would be simple to find out the truth. All I'd have to do is read a few palms or tea leaves."

Mr. Shinler and most of the councilmen stared at the new postmistress in disbelief.

Tootie was the first to speak. "We don't need any of your hocus-pocus stuff to prove that my father is innocent!"

"My daughter's right!" Eve said to Mrs. Deuce. Then she turned and looked around at the crowd. "I can't believe you're accusing Donald of robbing the bank! If you want information about where he's gone, I'll gladly give it to you. He and Pearl have gone back to St. Paul,

Minnesota—that's where we're from. Some simple checking will prove Donald's innocence."

"Let's call the sheriff from Webster," one of the councilmen suggested again. "He'll get to the bottom of this."

The Shinler Mercantile was the only place for such a call, and the bulk of the people started pushing into the store. Sylvia joined them. Even Tootie's mother hurried along, all the while giving out information.

Why is Mother telling them all those details? They should trust us!

Just then Julius Deuce hollered, "Whoever wants a ride, get in and sit down! This bus is leaving."

"Wait!" Mrs. Deuce suddenly yelled. She hurried to the bus, waving a large package high in the air. As she panted up the steps, she said to her son, "Your package arrived today. You can add another one to your collection." And she handed Julius a parcel wrapped in brown paper.

Tootie knew everyone must be staring at her and Buddy. She didn't even want to see Arl or the Roy boys. Tootie put her arm around her brother and turned him away from the bus.

"Are you all right, Buddy Boy?" she asked, brushing some of the dirt off his coat.

"Toot?" Buddy questioned, obviously confused about everything that had happened. He laid his small round head into the crook of Tootie's neck.

Tootie tried her best to soothe her brother, but her mind was filled with a whirlwind of feelings.

A few minutes later, Eve came out of the store with

a sack of groceries. Buddy had calmed down considerably. It was obvious that he hadn't really been hurt in the ordeal—only frightened. Buddy picked up the handle of the wagon and began pulling the groceries.

"You mustn't get so riled," Mother said to Tootie after they'd left the outskirts of town. "No matter what people say or do, your temper should stay in check."

Tootie couldn't believe it. "But—"

"No 'buts'. You've been taught better than that. Today, after Father and Pearl left, I got out my Bible." There was a catch in Mother's throat as she talked.

Tootie looked over at her mother. There were tears running down her cheeks.

"I read a verse in the fourteenth chapter of John," Eve continued. "It helped me a lot. I wrote it down." Mother pulled a scrap of paper from her coat pocket and began to read. "Peace I leave with you, my peace I give unto you; not as the world giveth, give I unto you. Let not your heart be troubled, neither let it be afraid."

Once again, hot tears stung Tootie's eyes. *How can I have peace with everything that's happening?*

"I want us both to memorize this Bible verse," Mother continued. "I think we're going to need it in the days ahead. Here, read it to me."

Tootie took the paper, but she didn't want to. All she wanted to do was to go back to the Shinler Mercantile and make Sylvia and her father take back every word they'd said!

It was a miserable two-mile walk down the country road. Tootie slowed her steps even more because she did not want to get to their farmhouse and find it empty.

"Why didn't they wait to say good-bye?" Tootie finally asked.

"I'm sorry, lass. Your father just couldn't bear to see your sad face. He asked me to say it for him."

"What about Pearl?"

Eve sighed. "You know your sister. Pearl couldn't wait to get back to the city. This is probably the best thing for her. She'll have to find work, along with your father."

Tootie wondered where Pearl and her father would live. She still couldn't believe they had actually gone.

Mother interrupted Tootie's thoughts. "Don't worry about the Shinlers and the others. They will soon realize your father is innocent."

They'd better! Tootie thought and clenched her fists.

Finally they came to the palm reading sign in front of Mrs. Deuce's house. "I saw this sign earlier on my way into town," Eve commented. "Then when that woman suggested she could help solve the robbery by reading palms, I knew this must be her place."

"It is," Tootie said. "Her name's Mrs. Deuce."

"I can't believe we have someone involved in the occult living right here in Siren!" Mother exclaimed.

"What's the occult?"

Eve looked at Tootie. "It's magical arts and practices. You know, things having to do with the devil."

Chills ran over Tootie's body. "Oh, Mama! I don't think Mrs. Deuce is really a partner with the devil. Good grief, she's a postmistress! I think this palm reading stuff is just some silly hocus-pocus game."

Eve shook her head. "You can't be too careful, lass. The next thing we'll hear is that the woman reads tarot cards. Now that's serious business. And it's certainly not a game or a hobby!"

Tootie had never heard of tarot cards before, but she didn't want to waste any more time talking about Mrs. Deuce.

They turned off the main road and headed down the side road to their farm. Buddy was having trouble pulling the wagon over the rough ground.

"Here, let me help," Tootie offered. She straightened the sack of flour and the few canned goods which were in the wagon. Then she took the handle from Buddy. He ran ahead in his clumsy manner.

Tootie said, "That stupid Sylvia Shinler could've hurt him! She's so mean!"

Eve shook her head. "You're right—she is mean. But you shouldn't call her names."

Tootie mumbled something under her breath. Then she decided it would be best to change the subject. "He doesn't know about Father and Pearl, does he?" Tootie whispered, nodding her head toward Buddy.

"No." Eve sadly shook her head. "Even if I'd tried to explain, Buddy wouldn't understand. Instead, I've tried to keep him busy all day. That's another reason for this long walk. I wanted to get him away from the farm."

Tootie yanked the wagon roughly. "Somebody's got to tell him!"

Eve didn't say a word.

Tootie noticed the deep lines between and around her mother's eyes. And for the first time she thought her mother looked old. Even her hair seemed more gray.

Eve turned and caught Tootie staring. "God will work all this out," Mother reassured. "He's done it in the past; he will do it again."

Tootie wished she had the faith of her mother.

It wasn't long before they reached the farmhouse. Buddy had been running in and out of the house and even out to the barn. Tootie and Mother stopped by the tamarack tree and watched his frantic search.

"Da! Da! Da!" Buddy hollered.

Tootie's heart ached and tears came to her eyes.

Just as Tootie was about to say something, Mother began to quote the Bible verse about peace. She got a few of the words mixed up. But the more Eve tried to quote the verse, the angrier Tootie became.

"Peace!" Tootie shouted. "How can anyone have peace at a time like this?"

Eve looked at her in surprise, but before she could scold her daughter, Tootie marched off, leaving the wagon and groceries behind.

"Come on, Buddy," she yelled. "You and I have chores to do."

It was soon obvious that Buddy wasn't interested in doing chores. Even stacking wood didn't draw his attention away from searching for his father.

"Come and help me milk Babe." Tootie grabbed her brother's hand and started toward the barn. But neither Babe nor the milking could bring a smile to Buddy's quivering lips.

Finally Tootie held her brother squarely by his slumped shoulders and looked lovingly into his eyes. "Da Da is gone," she said slowly.

Buddy stared at her.

"Da Da is gone," Tootie repeated. This time she motioned with her arm, indicating Father had left the farm.

Buddy's shoulders sagged even more. When Tootie saw the sad flicker of understanding begin to dawn in Buddy's almond-shaped eyes, she couldn't stand it. She had to say something more.

"Da Da and Pearl went to the city, but they will come back. They will come back!"

Buddy pulled away. "Da! Da! Da!" he hollered. He searched the barn again, and he kept walking around the spot where the truck had been parked. "Da! Da! Da!"

Tootie couldn't bear to watch her brother. She figured he needed some time by himself. *Maybe if he stays in the barn long enough, he'll understand,* she thought. Tootie loaded her arms full of wood and hurried to the house.

When she came back to the barn for a second load, Buddy was nowhere in sight.

"Buddy Boy," Tootie hollered. "Come here. Where are you?"

But after making a thorough search of the barn and the yard, Tootie ran back into the house. "Mama, I can't find Buddy!" Tootie cried in a panic.

"Oh, he can't have gone far. I'll help you look." Mother put down the pot she was carrying and grabbed her coat. The search for Buddy turned into a nightmare for Tootie. She couldn't believe all this was happening. She yelled and yelled as she and Mother frantically searched everywhere. It was getting dark, and Mother lit two kerosene lanterns. While they were looking in the shrubs along the side of the house, Tootie and her mother heard some whimpering.

"Shush!" Eve said. "Listen."

There it was again!

"That's Buddy," Tootie whispered. Her heart was pounding wildly. She pointed to the trapdoor on the root cellar. It was slightly ajar.

Mother nodded and explained in a whisper, "I must've left it open after I stored our canned goods."

Tootie pulled up the leaning door, and there down in

the cellar was Buddy. He was huddled in the darkness, sobbing.

Mother held the lantern high. Buddy cowered farther away.

"Oh, Buddy Boy!" Tootie gasped. She handed her lantern to Mother and took the two steps down into the cellar. "Come here, you sweet boy," she said and hurried to Buddy's side. She got down on the dirt floor and pulled him close. "Go ahead and cry," she whispered into his ear. "Just cry and cry and get it all out."

Tootie wanted to do the same, but she knew she had to be strong for her little brother.

Buddy nestled his head in the crook of Tootie's neck and kept sobbing.

Mother leaned down into the cellar with the lanterns. "Bring him up here," she said. "The cold down there can't be good for him."

The least of his worries is the cold, Tootie thought. She looked around the small, underground cellar which was stocked sparingly with food. Suddenly the thought of Sylvia Shinler's cellar with enough food to feed the entire state of Wisconsin came to Tootie's mind. Quickly she began to help Buddy to his feet. "Come on. Let's get out of here!"

The cellar was too low to allow them to stand up straight. Crouching down, she helped Buddy up the two steps and out into the chilly evening air.

Later that night, Tootie lay in the double bed she had shared with Pearl. It was different having the bed to herself, and she wasn't sure she was going to like it. Buddy was across the room in his bed, sound asleep. He was snoring loudly.

She thought over the long evening of rocking, cuddling, singing softly, and doing just about everything she and Mother could think of to comfort little Buddy. It took hours to calm him down, but finally he ate a few spoonfuls of soup before going to bed.

Ever so quietly Tootie slipped out from the covers and knelt by her bedside, shivering as her bare knees hit the cold braided rug. "Oh, God," Tootie whispered, "you said you would give us peace. Well, none of us have any." She stopped praying and looked over toward her sleeping brother. "What's going to happen to my Buddy Boy? That stupid Sylvia Shinler won't leave us alone! She pushes Buddy down in the dirt and calls Daddy a robber! She's so mean! I hate her!"

Suddenly Tootie wondered if she should tell that to God. Quickly she added, "But I am thankful you helped us find Buddy. And I am thankful that he didn't catch cold down in that cellar, and he's right here sound asleep. Please help Father and Pearl to get a good night's sleep, too. And please, please do something quick about finding the bank robber!"

She thought it would be hours before she could sleep, but immediately after finishing her prayer and getting back into bed, she began to relax. It felt strange. She stretched out on the saggy mattress. Before she could ponder further, she drifted into a restful sleep.

Before daybreak, Tootie opened her eyes. She felt rested and stretched out her arms and legs full length. Suddenly, it all came flooding back—Daddy and Pearl leaving to find jobs in the city, the robbery, the terrible accusations, and then Buddy hiding in the darkness of the root cellar. Tootie jumped up to check on her little brother.

He was sound asleep, and Tootie wanted him to stay that way. She grabbed her clothes and tiptoed out of the room.

Mother was already up and dressed. She was sitting at the kitchen table with a pencil in her hand and papers strewn about.

"Come here, lass," Eve said with enthusiasm and pulled out a chair for Tootie. "Look what I've been working on."

Tootie draped her clothes on the back of the chair and sat down.

"I've been making plans," Mother explained. Then she stopped and settled back in her chair. "I bet you'd

44

probably like to get dressed and have something to eat first."

"No," Tootie insisted. "Honest. Tell me what you're so excited about."

Eve leaned forward and pushed the papers closer to Tootie. "I've been planning how we're going to buy a pig. Maybe two. I've also been thinking about raising chickens. We'll have to build a brooder."

Tootie stared at the figures on the paper and then back at her mother.

"Don't be so surprised, lass."

"But we don't know anything about pigs or chickens! And what's a brooder?"

Eve smiled. "A brooder is a warm place where you raise baby chicks. And don't worry—we can learn everything we need to know. We'll ask questions. We'll study. We'll go to the library. In fact, I'm planning on walking there today."

"I could bring home some books from the school library," Tootie suggested.

"Good! Your father has promised to send us ten dollars every week. We're going to put that money to good use. And I've also decided we're taking out insurance on this old farm."

"We are?" Tootie questioned.

"Yes, I think that's the wise thing to do."

"What else have you thought about doing?" Tootie asked, half teasing. She leaned back and smiled at her mother.

Eve chuckled. "You're looking at me mighty strange,

young lady. But I'm serious. Now pay attention. You and I have to work together. This farm isn't going to flourish if we don't take charge of our situation. It's not going to be easy, but with God's help and a whole lot of hard work—we can do it!"

Tootie began to get excited. "You mean it, don't you?"

"I sure do! Also, we're going to have a garden—a big garden. It's already spring, and it will soon be time to plant."

"Don't we have to do something to get the ground ready?" Tootie asked, remembering comments she had overheard between the Roys and Arl.

"I'm sure there's plenty that needs to be done. We'll find out exactly what, and Buddy will get to work. He'll love it! Preparing the ground will be his responsibility. He can help with the planting and be the one to take care of weeds. He's become a good helper since we moved here to the farm. He's adjusted so well!"

Neither mentioned last night. The sight of her brother down in the cellar came to Tootie's mind. Then she had another thought. "If we grew some apple trees, we could store the apples in the cellar. They'd be great for pies. You're the best baker I know!"

"We'll have to check into that," Eve said and jotted a note down on the paper. "Maybe a cherry tree would also be a wise investment. Meanwhile we can grow strawberries and rhubarb in our garden. Maybe we can start by selling strawberry-rhubarb pies!"

"I'll help. Who knows, we might even open that bakery in town—the one that's out of business," Tootie reminded her mother.

Eve laughed. "Not so fast. One thing at a time. For now, you have a cow to milk. While you get dressed and do the chores, I'll make breakfast."

Tootie jumped up and gave her mother a big hug.

But the moment they finished their embrace and Tootie looked into the face of her mother, she saw a change. "What is it?" Tootie asked anxiously.

As though measuring every word, Eve said, "Tootie, today will probably be the worst day of your life. Some people in town may still accuse your father of being the bank robber."

Tootie backed away and set her jaw.

"Just a minute," Mother admonished. "Let me finish. Don't go losing that temper of yours. Everyone will soon find out that your father is innocent. The Webster sheriff is coming. He'll set people straight. Now, you promise me that you won't go fighting with anybody— not even Sylvia Shinler."

Tootie pressed her lips closed. She did not want to promise any such thing! She thought she was through with fighting, but after what Sylvia had said and done yesterday, Tootie wasn't so sure.

"Promise me," Mother demanded. "Besides, God wants us to be peacemakers and leave the vindicating to him. Now, promise me."

In a barely audible voice, Tootie mumbled, "I promise." Then she grabbed her clothes and ran from the room.

It took longer that morning to do the chores. All sorts of thoughts went round and round in Tootie's head as she milked Babe. But she had made that promise, and she knew she had to keep it.

Finally Tootie went to wake Buddy. She needed to help him get ready for the day. Besides, she wanted to see if Buddy was all right after his stay in the root cellar.

"Da! Da! Da!" Buddy said as he sat down at the breakfast table. He looked around at the empty places where Father and Pearl used to sit.

Tootie quickly wiped away her own tears with the back of her hand. Then she smiled at Buddy and tried her best to explain the changes she and Mother were planning to make on the farm. "We're going to buy a pig," she said. "And Mama wants lots of chickens. We're also going to have a garden!"

"And you're going to be the gardener!" Mother added. "I'll show you just what to do. It'll be fun."

Buddy grinned. Cereal dribbled from his chin. He couldn't understand what they were saying, but he sensed their excitement.

Tootie leaned over and planted a kiss on the tip of his nose. "We're going to work together, Buddy Boy. And you're going to be the best gardener this town has ever seen!"

"Toot! Toot! Toot!" Buddy said and clapped his hands.

Tootie wiped away another tear as she quickly made a bread-and-butter sandwich.

When she ran out the door for school, the Roy boys

were waiting for her near the big tree. "We believe your father's innocent," Lawrence said immediately.

"We sure do!" Lavern added with fervor. "I can't believe anyone would think your father would rob the bank!"

"Isn't it ridiculous!" Tootie said.

As they headed down the road, Leo asked, "Are you going to fight with Sylvia today?"

"Tootie's through with fighting," Lawrence said with a sly grin. "Remember?"

They all laughed as they hurried to the bus.

Arl was waiting for them, along with Mrs. Deuce. The postmistress started talking to them before they had time to say hello. "I'm going to be taking the school bus back and forth to work each day," she explained. "The town council agreed that would be fine."

"That's nice," Tootie responded.

Mrs. Deuce continued, "Julius got up awful early this morning to start the bus route. He's the strangest young man. It's almost amusing how excited he is over that collection of his."

"What collection?" Tootie asked. She thought this was the oddest conversation. *At least Mrs. Deuce isn't talking about the robbery or reading palms,* Tootie thought. *And she certainly doesn't look or sound like anyone involved with the devil!*

The postmistress kept on talking, ignoring Tootie's question. "He was fiddling with them again this morning." She pointed directly at Tootie. "You need to come over and see them sometime. He won't let me touch the dear things. I've got the strangest son!"

He's not the only strange one, Tootie thought. She looked at her friends and could tell they were thinking the same thing. Just then the bus came into view. As soon as Julius stopped, they piled onto the bus and down the aisle.

"What was all that about?" Arl asked quietly.

Tootie shrugged.

Lavern whispered, "Maybe her son collects tea leaves."

They all tried to stifle their laughter. They certainly didn't want Mrs. Deuce hearing them.

Before long Julius stopped the bus in front of Shinler Mercantile. Tootie dreaded seeing Sylvia. She didn't know how she was going to keep the promise she'd made to Mother if Sylvia said one more hateful thing.

Mr. Shinler hurried out of the store with Sylvia and her friends. He poked his head into the bus and said loudly to Mrs. Deuce, "Sheriff Collins came over from Webster last night. He'll be questioning everybody about that robbery. Probably come by the post office sometime this afternoon."

Mrs. Deuce nodded. "I could solve the case," she announced. "I've told you that before."

"So you've said," Mr. Shinler said with obvious irritation. "But we're serious about this!" Then he looked toward the back of the bus. "We'll find that Donald McCarthy real soon!"

Tootie jumped to her feet. They weren't going to start that again!

Mrs. Deuce rose to leave. "Don't be so sure of yourself, Mr. Shinler."

The storekeeper shook his finger. "That Donald McCarthy is guilty in my book!"

"In mine, too!" Sylvia said. She walked up the bus steps, passed Mrs. Deuce, and settled herself smugly into the seat the postmistress had left.

Tootie felt her entire body go hot with rage. It took all her willpower to stand there and stare at the smirk on Sylvia's face. Tootie balled her fists and clenched her jaw. If she hadn't made that promise, Tootie knew she would have stormed up the aisle and attacked Sylvia Shinler. And maybe even Sylvia's father! But a promise is a promise. Tootie bit her lower lip and slowly sat back down.

Arl looked at the Roy boys in amazement, but none of them dared say a word.

When they arrived at school, Mr. Brightenger began their class with an announcement. "The town council met last night. Sheriff Collins from Webster was in attendance. He's going to help us find out who robbed our bank." He stopped momentarily.

Tootie held her chin high and stared back silently at her teacher.

"Some people have already made some wild accusations. But I don't think that's proper. People are innocent until proven guilty."

Tootie was just about to turn and give a meaningful look at Sylvia when she remembered her mother's comment about being a peacemaker. *This is harder than fighting and getting even,* she thought. *It would be much easier to simply clobber her!*

Mr. Brightenger continued, "So, until this robbery is solved and we recover our money, we've got to do something. The town council decided to have a large fundraiser that will include all of Siren. The money collected will go as a reward to anyone who leads to the capture of the robber and the return of the money to the bank."

Everyone started talking. It sounded as though they were all planning to become private detectives.

"Tell us about the fund-raiser, Mr. Brightenger," one student urged. "Do you think it'll raise enough for a reward?"

"It should," their teacher continued. "Sheriff Collins agreed with us that a pie social would be a good idea. Besides, it will take everyone's mind off our tragedy."

"Pie socials are fun!" a student from the back of the room exclaimed.

"My mom hates them," Lawrence said suddenly.

Sylvia giggled. "That's because your dad can't tell which pie she baked, and he bids on the wrong one."

Several others giggled.

"Hold down the chatter," Mr. Brightenger said. "This is serious business. Sheriff Collins wants us to be warned. He absolutely does not want anyone taking chances just to get that reward money. Leave the heroics to him. The sheriff says that if you find out anything about the robbery or the bank money, don't get personally involved. Just tell him what you've discovered, and he'll carry the investigation from there. Understand? But meanwhile, we're going to plan this pie social."

"A pie social!" Tootie mumbled under her breath. "What is a pie social, anyway? It sounds ridiculous."

"What are you saying, Miss McCarthy?" their teacher asked.

"Nothing."

Mr. Brightenger persisted. "Have you ever been to a pie social before? They're common around these parts. I believe you, your mother, and that little brother of yours might enjoy it."

Tootie could tell her teacher was trying to be kind. But before she could answer, Sylvia piped up, "Tootie's from the city. She's probably never made a pie in her life! But I'm a great baker. I'm going to make the best pie anyone has ever seen or tasted. There'll be dozens of boys bidding on mine."

"Not if they know you made it," Tootie said half under her breath. But she'd said it too loud, because several students began to snicker.

"I bet you can't even bake a pie!" Sylvia demanded, red in the face.

Tootie was surprised that Sylvia didn't know her family had owned a bakery business before moving to Siren. She'd been so nosey about everything else.

Tootie didn't answer. She'd promised her mother. Besides, she had more important things on her mind than silly old pies!

The following days were filled with new developments. Sheriff Collins had questioned almost everyone in Siren. He mentioned to many that he had been in contact several times over the phone with Tootie's father in St. Paul, Minnesota. He said that it could be proven that Donald was already out of town when the bank robbery occurred. And at the last town council meeting Sheriff Collins reported that he had investigated the entire McCarthy family and found them above reproach. He was convinced that Donald McCarthy was totally innocent of the crime.

After the meeting, some of the councilmen apologized to Eve for being so quick to judge her husband. A few began going out of their way to do simple deeds of kindness to make up for their cruel words. However, not one word of apology was forthcoming from Mr. Shinler nor from Sylvia.

Even though it had been hard, Tootie was truly thankful she had obeyed her mother and had not gotten into a fight with Sylvia.

It was still a mystery to all that there were no clues

whatsoever about the bank robber. Some people were saying that Sheriff Collins must have some idea who the robbers were but that he was keeping the information to himself.

Meanwhile, life on the McCarthy farm became a whirl of activity. The weather was getting warmer, and every day after school Tootie helped Buddy turn over the soil in preparation for planting their garden. They had already purchased several packets of seeds. Every purchase came with lots of advice from the townsfolk. They informed Tootie and her mother on how deep, exactly when, and where to plant.

Buddy was enjoying the hard work, and he smiled more as the week progressed. One afternoon Tootie did find him crying in the barn, but besides that he had adjusted surprisingly well to the absence of Father and Pearl. *He's doing better than me,* Tootie thought.

It wasn't until the end of the second week that Tootie and Eve had time to study the books Tootie had brought home from the school library. They were learning about brooders and how one should be built. Several men had volunteered to help, including Mr. Roy and his sons.

Tootie kept her finger in the book she was reading to mark her place. Then she looked thoughtfully at her mother. "What's the matter, Mama? You're so quiet tonight."

"I can't believe your father hasn't written," Eve replied with a frown between her deep-set eyes. "I'm glad Sheriff Collins reported that your father and Pearl are both doing well. And it was wonderful to hear about that auditing job your father found and how the church families are helping with a place to stay. But I still think he should've written us by now."

Tootie knew her mother had already taken out insurance on the farm, but was waiting for that first ten dollars from Father before she purchased supplies for the brooder. "We'll probably hear tomorrow," Tootie said encouragingly. She hoped they would—besides she was anxious to know if Pearl had found a job.

"You're probably right," Eve admitted and patted Tootie's hand. "Here I am always telling you not to worry—and now look at me. I guess I should take some of my own advice."

Tootie smiled broadly. Then she picked up the book and continued reading out loud to her mother.

Meanwhile, the excitement around Siren over the upcoming pie social seemed ridiculous to Tootie. It was mentioned every day, but Tootie ignored the talk and gave her time and energy to the changes at the farm.

The tension between Tootie and Sylvia continued to increase. Tootie tried to stay her distance, but her terrible feelings toward Sylvia seemed to grow deeper by the day. Tootie constantly heard Sylvia whispering about the robbery and how Tootie's father must somehow be involved.

On Friday afternoon after school Julius stopped the bus as usual in front of Shinler Mercantile. Mrs. Deuce hurried over. "Miss McCarthy," she yelled. "I know you and your mother have been anxiously awaiting this.

You'll find in here what you need." She held up an envelope and waved it high in the air.

Tootie walked up the aisle and took the letter.

"It's from your father," Mrs. Deuce explained. And then she added, "He's finally sent you and your mother that money you've been expecting!"

"What money?" Sylvia asked suspiciously. "I know where he got it! It's probably from our bank!"

"Don't start that again!" Tootie responded hotly.

"Well, you started it," Sylvia sneered.

As Tootie marched back to the rear seat, she had to pass Sylvia. It took all of her strength not to shove Sylvia out of the way.

But the moment Tootie sat down and looked at her letter, another thought suddenly came to her mind. *How did Mrs. Deuce know Mother and I were waiting for this money?*

Tootie stared at the envelope. It was sealed. She opened it carefully and peeked inside. There in the folded page of Father's letter was their first ten-dollar bill!

"Are you all right?" Arl asked. "You look like you've seen a ghost."

"Oh, it's that Mrs. Deuce. I think she must have some secret method of reading mail through sealed envelopes! How did she know we were expecting this letter from Daddy?"

"That's easy," Arl said. "Even I knew that you and your mother were anxious to hear from him."

Lavern leaned over the seat. "So did we. Anyway, aren't you ever going to fight with Sylvia?"

58

Suddenly Tootie relaxed. "You'd love that, wouldn't you?"

Lawrence shoved his brother. "Quit your teasing. I think Tootie's new strategy is making Sylvia even madder."

Tootie hadn't thought about having a new strategy. She was simply trying to keep her promise to Mother.

Then Lawrence asked, "Are you going tomorrow night to the pie social?"

"I don't think so," Tootie responded.

"You've got to," he pleaded. "Everyone will be there. All the money raised will help with that reward money. Besides, it'll be fun. My folks could stop and pick you up."

Tootie couldn't resist. "I'll ask," she promised.

The minute Tootie got home, she mentioned the pie social.

"That'd be nice," Eve said. "We'll all go. It's time we took a break. Besides, Buddy will love it."

Early Saturday morning, Mother, Tootie, and Buddy went to the root cellar to check their supplies and decide what kind of pie to bake. It was the first time Buddy had been in the cellar since the night he'd hidden and cried in the dark.

"We have lard, flour, and sugar," Mother announced, trying to keep the conversation on a light note. "And look here, we still have these last cans of fillings left over from the bakery. We have our choice of squash, apple, or cherry. Which will it be?"

"Let's make all three," Tootie said and smiled at Buddy. "You'd love a day of baking pies, wouldn't you?"

Buddy clapped his hands.

Tootie had missed the smell of pies baking. She remembered the delicious odors that had wafted up to their apartment above the bakery. "Baking pies always gives me a homey feeling," she said as she and Buddy stacked the supplies in their arms and carried them into the house.

Their baking day turned out to be a lot of fun. It was almost like old times, except Father and Pearl were missing. They rolled out dough on floured boards, carefully placed the thin pastry into deep-dish pie tins, and filled each one almost to overflowing. Tootie fluted the flaky edges; then Mother pricked a pretty design into the top crust. Buddy kept the stove fire burning, while constantly nibbling as he worked.

By the time they finished, six pies were placed carefully into a big box that Mother had saved from their move. Mr. Brightenger had given instructions on how to label the pies. Tootie wrote their names on scraps of paper and slipped them under the pies. Her name was under three, and Eve's under the other three. Then she covered the box with several dish towels.

At six o'clock the Roy family arrived. Mother hurried into the front seat next to Mrs. Roy, while Tootie and Buddy got into the open back of the truck next to Lavern, Lawrence, and Leo. It was a windy ride into town, but it didn't take long to get to Shinler Mercantile. The social was to be held in the town hall above.

The Roy boys darted off the minute the truck stopped. Mother took Buddy by the hand. Then she looked at

Tootie. "Take the pies where they belong; then go find your friends. I want you to enjoy your evening."

Tootie gratefully picked up the box. She was walking through the Mercantile toward the back steps that led to the town hall, when she heard Sylvia's voice. She was talking in hushed tones to someone in the next aisle. They were hidden from Tootie's view.

"I baked a beautiful pie," Sylvia bragged. "You want to know what kind it is?"

The person must have shaken his head, because Sylvia continued. "Come on, I could give you a clue. That way you could bid on mine, and we could eat together."

Who in the world is Sylvia coaxing? Tootie wondered. She thought of sneaking around to find out, when all of a sudden she heard Arl's voice. "That would be cheating, Sylvia. Besides—"

Tootie hurried up the steps before she heard anymore. She'd had absolutely no idea that Sylvia liked Arl.

Tootie had just put the pies on the table when Mrs. Deuce came and stood beside her. "That's not the only surprise you'll discover tonight. I was looking into my crystal ball this afternoon. I saw that tonight is going to be a landmark for Siren. This will be their best fund-raiser ever. And do you want to hear how you are involved?"

"No!" Tootie said forcefully. "I don't want to hear any more of your predictions. Besides, I don't believe in all this hocus-pocus stuff."

"You should," the postmistress said undisturbed. "Others do. My first customer is coming tomorrow."

"Who?" Tootie asked.

Mrs. Deuce didn't answer. She just grinned.

Tootie didn't want to stand there a second longer. Quickly she turned and hurried away.

But as the evening progressed, Tootie forgot all about Mrs. Deuce. Mr. Brightenger was selected to be the auctioneer. His cough was completely gone and he looked in good health as he stood on the small raised platform in front of the crowd. He picked up a pie from the table and held it high in the air.

"Who will bid on this beauty?" he began. Most of the folks from Siren were there and also a large group from Webster.

"I'll bid one dollar!" one man shouted.

"Who'll give me two?" Mr. Brightenger challenged.

"Two!" another man shouted quickly.

"Three!" the first man demanded. "That's my wife's pie."

Everyone laughed. It was fun to watch the men and boys do the bidding, and then to discover who had actually baked the pie. The one who got the bid had to eat the pie with the one who baked it.

The fact that Tootie and her mother had brought three pies each completely confused the bidding. As Mr. Brightenger displayed their pies one by one, the bids went higher and higher. Before long, Eve, Tootie, and Buddy had a semicircle of top bidders surrounding them enjoying every bite of their delicious squash, apple, and cherry pies.

"This is the best squash pie I've ever eaten," one man admitted.

"You should try this cherry," another suggested.

There were a few comments from disgruntled wives and girlfriends, but most were good sports—except for Sylvia. The moment Arl bid on one of Tootie's pies, Sylvia became obviously angry. She stood with her hands on her hips, glaring at Tootie. Arl took the pie and joined the semicircle of satisfied bidders.

"Tootie McCarthy, you cheated!" Sylvia challenged loudly. "You stole those pies just like your father stole that bank money. You're a bunch of cheaters."

"Quiet!" Mr. Shinler scolded.

Sylvia ran from the room.

Tootie was furious. How could Sylvia say that in front of the whole town!

A number of people looked embarrassed. But after a few seconds, someone chuckled and mentioned something about jealousy. No one seemed to have any problem at all sluffing off Sylvia's comment. Even Arl seemed undisturbed. He winked at Tootie as he bit into his second piece of pie.

Later that evening, by the time the last pie had been auctioned, $252.00 had been raised. Many of the people were crediting the success of the fund-raiser directly to Tootie and her mother.

Mr. Brightenger hurried over to them. "This has been the best pie social our town has ever seen. You two have certainly made a landmark in Siren tonight!"

Tootie sucked in her breath. Those were the exact words that Mrs. Deuce had predicted before the evening began!

Tootie had a hard time going to sleep that night. She still felt angry over Sylvia's comment at the pie social. And then the whole business concerning Mrs. Deuce's prediction really bothered her. *How did she know? Can Mrs. Deuce really predict what's going to happen?* For the first time Tootie wondered if the postmistress really did possess some special powers.

Stretching out in the double bed, Tootie went back over the entire evening. She couldn't believe $252.00 had been raised as a result of the pie social. "Two hundred and fifty-two dollars," Tootie said out loud.

Buddy was sound asleep on the other side of the room.

"I want that reward money," Tootie whispered to the sound of Buddy's snores. "That means I've got to find out who the robber is. I've got to prove Father had nothing to do with it. And I've got to find out where all that stolen money is hidden."

It seemed apparent to everyone in Siren that Sheriff Collins was not any closer to finding out the truth about the robbery than when he first began the investigation.

I'm going to have to solve this mystery on my own, Tootie thought. *We need that reward money.*

Suddenly Mrs. Deuce's grinning face seemed to loom over her. Tootie could almost hear the postmistress whisper, "You too can be one of my customers. I can look into my crystal ball. I can tell you who robbed that bank. I can help you find the stolen money so you will win that reward."

"Be quiet!" Tootie said out loud.

"What is it?" Mother asked as she passed the bedroom door. "Who are you talking to?"

"No one," Tootie admitted, feeling foolish. "My imagination is running wild tonight."

Eve chuckled. "You'd best get some sleep. I asked Mr. and Mrs. Roy if they would mind picking us up for church in the morning. We'll need to do the chores before we go."

"Good night," Tootie said and turned over, determined to shove Mrs. Deuce and Sylvia right out of her mind.

The next morning while milking Babe, Tootie wondered about the new minister who had just been hired. The church committee had been looking for a pastor for almost a year. Finally, one man had agreed to come, Pastor Edward J. Underhill. There had been a lot of talk about Pastor Underhill's qualifications. Some thought he was too highly qualified for such a small, country community. Others expressed concern about how the dwindling congregation could afford to pay him. But the reports of the minister's humility had won the vote. Tootie and her mother were excited that the church in Siren would have its own minister.

Tootie carried the bucket of milk into the house. "I've missed going to church," Tootie said to her mother as she carefully scooped off the cream.

"Me, too," Eve admitted. "I'm looking forward to hearing a message from God's Word."

"God, God, God," Buddy said and clapped his hands.

Tootie laughed as she put aside the heavy cream, which later she would churn into butter, and poured her brother a tall glass of milk. "You're always so happy," she said to her brother, "especially when it comes to God."

"God! God! God!" Buddy repeated excitedly.

"You little scalawag," Tootie said with endearment as she tenderly wiped the milk mustache off Buddy's upper lip. "We need to hurry and get you dressed for church."

At ten o'clock the Roys arrived. The McCarthys hurried out to the truck. Tootie helped Buddy into the back and then jumped up to join him and the Roy boys. Buddy's excitement grew as once again they bounced over the rough road toward town.

The morning was bright and beautiful. The longer Tootie stayed in the country, the more she felt at home. *If only Father and Pearl were here!* Once again Tootie thought of the $252.00 reward. *If I get that reward money, they will come back home. We will be together as a family!* Her determination grew to solve the mystery of the bank robbery.

It wasn't long before they arrived at church and Mr. Roy stopped in the graveled parking area. Immediately

Tootie noticed that the sign in front of the church had been fixed. It said one word—WELCOME. It had been hanging at an angle ever since the McCarthys moved to Siren. The church was still in need of several coats of paint, but fixing the sign was a big improvement.

The sanctuary was already crowded when they entered. The service was about to start and people were still trying to find places to sit.

Lawrence whispered, "It seems like everyone in town is interested in hearing the new minister. Church hasn't been this full in over a year."

"Do you see Mrs. Deuce?" Tootie asked.

Lawrence looked surprised. "Of course not. I wouldn't expect to see her in church."

Then Tootie scanned the audience to see if Sylvia was present. She spotted Arl toward the front. He was sitting with little Olof Olson. Olof waved excitedly to Buddy.

"Olof! Olof! Olof!" Buddy said and clapped his hands.

"Shush!" Tootie admonished. She led her brother by the hand as they followed Mother and the usher to one of the back pews.

Just then, from the side door near the platform, the new minister entered. He was in his early forties, tall, trim, and had a receding hairline. Tootie liked the way he smiled and nodded his head toward individuals in the congregation.

Mr. Brightenger had been sitting in one of the two chairs on the platform. He walked forward and stood behind the pulpit. "Please rise," he said, motioning with his hands. "Pastor Underhill has asked me to lead you in an opening hymn. Turn to page 135 in your hymnals." The organist played a short introduction and then the congregation began to sing. The song was new to Tootie so instead of trying to sing along, she concentrated on the words.

When peace, like a river, attendeth my way,
When sorrows like sea billows roll;
Whatever my lot, Thou hast taught me to say,
"It is well, it is well with my soul."

The words of the song reminded Tootie of the Bible verse about peace that she and Mother had discussed. Tootie could feel her mother looking at her, but Tootie continued staring at Mr. Brightenger as he led the song.

Life without Father and Pearl was lonely. Tootie had tried to keep busy. She was enjoying the challenge on the farm—but she definitely wouldn't say she had *peace*. And then there was Sylvia. *With her around there's never any peace!* Tootie thought. *Not to mention that fortune-telling, crystal-ball-reading Mrs. Deuce! I bet the person who wrote this song didn't have all these people to deal with.*

With a troubled heart, Tootie listened as the congregation repeated the song for a second time.

Then the congregation sat down, and Pastor Underhill stood to preach. As in the reports, the one characteristic that stood out above all others was the humble, almost meek look in the Pastor's eyes. He smiled lovingly at the people before him.

"I was reading this week about the story behind this hymn," he began. "These words were written as an expression of faith in God's mysterious providence. Let me tell you the story."

Tootie sat on the edge of her seat.

"You see, a man by the name of H. G. Spafford had received the awful news that all four of his daughters had drowned at sea. They were on a ship that went down in a storm. Not one of his daughters had been spared. Mr. Spafford grieved and grieved until he could bear it no longer. He decided he needed to take a ship and go out to the very spot where his four daughters had lost their lives. That is exactly what he did. And as the captain slowed the vessel and stopped over the very spot of the tragedy, this father stood alone on deck. He gripped the railing and stared out over the waves that had swallowed his beautiful girls."

Tootie held her breath. She could almost feel this father's agony. *In a way, I've lost part of my family, too,* Tootie thought.

Pastor Underhill continued, "Suddenly an overwhelming peace flooded Mr. Spafford's soul. With tear-stained cheeks, this grieving father whispered to his heavenly Father, 'It is well, it is well with my soul.' Then he penned the words you have just sung. Listen, as I repeat them slowly. And if you have unrest in your soul, give that unrest to Jesus today."

Pastor Underhill repeated the words of the song, and

Tootie's knuckles turned white as she clasped her hands tightly in her lap. She wanted to say, "It is well, it is well with my soul," but she couldn't. It wasn't true. *If I could find out who robbed the bank without Mrs. Deuce's help and get that reward money, it would be true,* Tootie thought. *If Daddy and Pearl come home, it would be true. And if Sylvia left town, my soul would sing!* Her hatred toward Sylvia seemed to mount.

Just then the pastor said, "If you do not deal with your anger over a situation—you become the prisoner. That's right. As long as you hate your enemy, a jail door is closed and a prisoner is taken. And that prisoner is you."

Tootie held her breath. It was as though Pastor Edward J. Underhill had read her thoughts and was talking directly to her.

"Will harboring the anger solve the problem?" he continued. "Will getting even remove the hurt? Does hatred do any good? The father who penned the hymn had to release his hurt and his anger. And so do you. And when you do, you are the one released."

It didn't make sense. Tootie continued in her struggle until the sermon ended. She wasn't any closer to a solution as she headed out the church door and shook hands with Pastor Underhill. She wanted to ask him what she should do with her anger and hatred toward Sylvia, and also her growing fear of Mrs. Deuce and her powers. But no one else was talking about the pastor's sermon; they were all discussing the weather.

"The sky looks strange," Mr. Roy said with his wife

at his side. They both shook hands with the new minister. "This looks and feels like twister weather to me," Mr. Roy continued. "You may be in for quite a welcome!"

"Twister?" Pastor Underhill repeated. "Do you mean a tornado?"

"That's right," Mr. Brightenger said anxiously as he joined the circle of parishioners. "We've studied about them in my classroom, and I've tried to warn my students so they would be as prepared as possible. They all know what they should do in case of such an emergency." Then Mr. Brightenger stepped out into the sunlight and looked around him. "This is twister weather all right!"

Several councilmen interrupted the conversation. One said, "Don't mind them, preacher. Some people are always worrying."

"That's right," another added. "A twister hasn't hit these parts in years. In fact, I bet they couldn't tell you how long ago it's been."

Tootie took Buddy by the hand and walked him over to the Roys' truck. The weather looked fine to her. She figured the townspeople didn't know what else to talk about with their new minister, and this was easy conversation. Tootie looked down Main Street toward Shinler Mercantile. She wondered if Sylvia ever came to church. *Am I a prisoner because of my hatred?* she wondered, still pondering the words of the sermon.

Eve walked over and joined Tootie. "You're looking mighty thoughtful, lass. Does all this talk about twisters worry you?"

Tootie looked at her mother. "No, I've just been thinking about something else."

Eve smiled gently. "I miss them too, lass."

"Oh, Mother, if I could find that bank robber and get that reward—everything would be great. Daddy and Pearl would come home!"

"No heroics, Tootie," Eve warned. "You be careful. We're doing just fine without that reward money."

"But I want Daddy and Pearl to come home," Tootie responded.

"Da! Da! Da!" Buddy said with sudden tears in his eyes.

"Don't cry, Buddy Boy," Tootie said soothingly.

But Buddy started to sob.

It wasn't until Buddy got into the back of the Roy family's pickup that he began to calm down. Tootie knew she should be more careful with what she said around her brother.

Tootie listened to Lavern, Lawrence, and Leo as they settled themselves beside her and Buddy. They sounded like their father in their concern over the weather and the possibility of a twister coming through Siren.

Lawrence said, "Did you know that a twister drove a piece of straw right into the trunk of a tree?"

"I heard that one," Lavern responded. "But did you hear how a cow was picked up and then found more than ten miles away in another farmer's field? The cow wasn't even hurt. She was mooing contentedly as if nothing had happened."

Leo laughed. "Hey, my story is better than that. Did you hear—"

They were approaching the spot in the road where they turned onto the side road to their farms. Tootie knocked on the back of the truck. Mr. Roy was slowing to make the turn. He pulled to a stop when he heard the knocking.

"What is it?" he hollered, with a frown on his face.

Tootie jumped off the back of the truck. "Can I walk home from here?" she asked her mother.

Eve looked at Tootie with understanding in her eyes. "I'm sure that would be fine," she said. "I'll get something fixed for dinner, and Buddy can do some of the chores. Don't be too long."

"But the weather," Mrs. Roy nervously interrupted.

Eve smiled. "Tootie will be fine. It's not very far to the house. Besides, sometimes twisters can come in the heart. And just spending some time alone can help."

An understanding look spread across Mrs. Roy's face.

"What in the world are you women talking about?" Mr. Roy asked. He shook his head and looked at his wife. Then he looked at Eve and Tootie as though they didn't have a brain between the three of them. "Women folks," he grunted.

Tootie waved at Buddy and the Roy boys as the truck turned the corner and headed for home. She was standing directly next to the palm reading sign. She glanced over toward Mrs. Deuce's. And what Tootie saw took her completely by surprise.

Mrs. Deuce was standing by her back door motioning toward her. "Come here," she called in a pleasant tone. "Come over here for a few minutes."

Tootie didn't know what to do. She had always tried to be polite to adults, but Mrs. Deuce was different. Besides, Tootie wanted to be alone and do some serious thinking.

"I have chores to do," Tootie said. "I really should get going."

"Nonsense," the postmistress replied. "You jumped out of that truck right in front of my house for a purpose. I've been standing here waiting for my customer—who is late I might add. I have nothing better to do. And Julius is gone for the afternoon. So this meeting of ours must be fate."

Tootie took a step back.

Mrs. Deuce laughed, showing her white teeth. "There's nothing to fear. I know that since the reward money is up to two hundred and fifty-something, you have decided to solve the mystery about who robbed the bank on your own. That's what is on your mind. You want to clear your father's name once and for all. And you want that reward money so your father and sister can return home and live with you on the farm."

Tootie gasped. "How did you know all that?"

"Oh, I know even more—much more. If you come into my house and let me look into my crystal ball, it will reveal to us many secrets. I can help you solve this mystery."

In her heart, Tootie knew she should turn and run. But the idea of Mrs. Deuce looking into a crystal ball and finding answers to this robbery was beginning to sound fascinating. *I don't want her to use the crystal ball,* Tootie thought, *but I would love to just see it. What harm could that do?*

Tootie stared at the woman before her in the simple patterned housedress. *Besides, she doesn't look evil.* Tootie took a few steps closer to Mrs. Deuce.

The postmistress stretched out her hand in welcome. "I know that Shinler girl is your enemy," Mrs. Deuce confided. "I can give you advice on how to handle her. I can instruct you on how to focus your anger and do her much harm."

Tootie tried to push Pastor Underhill's sermon out of her mind. She vaguely remembered something about the danger of harboring anger. But the idea of doing harm to Sylvia seemed so much more enticing. Even the song about peace no longer rang in Tootie's ears. She hesitated only slightly.

"I can see that you are still uneasy," Mrs. Deuce said.

"Let's forget the crystal ball for now," she suggested. "If you want, we can do that later. Just come inside for a few minutes and let me show you my son's collection. It's fascinating."

Tootie had wondered about Julius's collection ever since Mrs. Deuce had mentioned it a couple of weeks ago. "All right, but I can't stay long," Tootie reminded her as she stepped over the threshold into the post-mistress's house.

To Tootie's surprise, the room looked bright and pleasant—not at all dark and dreary as she had imagined. She took a couple of steps farther into the room.

Mrs. Deuce's grin broadened.

But Tootie didn't notice. She had spotted row upon row of delicate dolls sitting proudly on white-painted shelves along the far wall of the front room. "These are beautiful!" Tootie exclaimed as she hurried over to take a closer look.

Each doll had a porcelain head and a cloth body, and was dressed in the most gorgeous little clothes Tootie had ever seen. Their white china faces were painted in soft muted colors.

"I've never seen any dolls like these before!" Tootie looked at one in particular that wore a lacy red-and-yellow dress. She reached out to touch it.

"Don't you touch!" Mrs. Deuce's voice came out in a screech. "Julius is very protective of his precious dolls. He doesn't even allow me to touch them. He'd know for sure if one was moved slightly from its place."

Tootie backed away from the rows of dolls and pursed

her lips. She couldn't imagine a grown man having a doll collection. Folding her arms, she turned and looked at Mrs. Deuce.

The postmistress chuckled. "I can see from your look that you don't approve. Well, as a matter of fact, neither do I. It's an odd collection for a man. But what's a mother to do? Julius spends his own money on the silly things. He watches over them like a hawk. If one is touched, he knows."

"What does he do with them?" Tootie asked.

"Nothing, absolutely nothing. He just sits and looks at them all lined up as pretty as can be. Odd," Mrs. Deuce admitted, shaking her head. "Julius is an odd young man. Sometimes I worry about him."

Tootie certainly agreed that he was strange, but she decided not to say so. Suddenly she wondered how he had lost his finger. She thought of asking, but knew it would be rude.

Just then they were interrupted by a knock on the door.

"That must be my customer!" Mrs. Deuce said with satisfaction. "Before we moved to Siren, I had quite a profitable business. But people here seem to be shy of me. Anyway, I'm sure my palm reading business will eventually catch on around these parts."

Tootie didn't think so, but she remained silent as Mrs. Deuce opened the door. And to Tootie's surprise, there on the front step stood her enemy, Sylvia Shinler.

"Holey moley!" Sylvia shouted the moment she saw Tootie. "What are you doing here?"

"Nothing!" Tootie shouted back, feeling embarrassed and ashamed at being caught in Mrs. Deuce's house.

Mrs. Deuce looked from one to the other. "You two are always at each other," she announced. Tootie thought she detected a note of satisfaction in the woman's voice.

Mrs. Deuce pointed toward the rows of dolls. "I was showing Miss McCarthy my son's doll collection," she explained.

Sylvia looked at the dolls and frowned. "That's ridiculous! Who ever heard of a grown man collecting dolls?" Then Sylvia turned on Tootie. "You came here to have your fortune told. You think you're so goody-goody, but I know better!"

Tootie knew in her heart that it wasn't only the dolls that had attracted her; it was Mrs. Deuce's ability to help her solve the bank robbery. *What a fool I've been! And then to be found out by Sylvia!* Tootie knew she'd never hear the end of this.

Sylvia sneered. "Well, looky here. For once Tootie doesn't have anything to say."

Tootie looked at Sylvia and said simply, "You're right. It was wrong of me to come. I don't have any excuse."

Sylvia stared at her as though she couldn't believe her ears. Even Mrs. Deuce looked startled.

"I should go," Tootie continued.

"I'm sure that would be wise," Mrs. Deuce agreed quickly. "Besides, I need to concentrate. I am going to get out my tarot cards and read them for Sylvia."

"Your what?" Tootie asked, suddenly remembering

her mother's comment about tarot cards being associated with the devil.

"My tarot cards," Mrs. Deuce repeated in an irritated tone.

Tootie began, "I don't want you to use those cards for Sylvia. My mother says—"

"Mind your own business," Sylvia interrupted. "Your mother has nothing to do with this! Just leave!"

"But you don't understand," Tootie tried to explain again.

"Leave!" both Sylvia and Mrs. Deuce demanded.

Tootie turned and marched out of the house. The temperature had risen and it felt like a hot summer's day. She headed down the side road toward her farm, mumbling under her breath. But she couldn't get Sylvia off her mind. Tootie knew beyond a doubt that Sylvia was in trouble. Mrs. Deuce's fortune-telling was no innocent game.

"It serves her right!" Tootie grumbled and kicked at the ground. "I tried to help." All the hateful and hurtful comments that Sylvia had said since Tootie moved to Siren came storming back into Tootie's mind.

"Sylvia deserves what she gets!" Tootie said out loud and kept walking.

But the farther she got from Mrs. Deuce's house, the worse she felt. *Maybe I should go back and try to warn Sylvia again,* Tootie thought. *That'd be crazy—she wouldn't listen to me! But I still should try,* Tootie kept arguing with herself.

Finally she stopped in the middle of the country road,

in front of the Olsons' farm, and prayed out loud. "Oh, God, what should I do?"

Immediately, she knew. She knew she had to go back. She knew she had to be the one to warn Sylvia. She knew she had to try to help, even if Sylvia got mad.

For a brief second Tootie thought of running over to the Olsons and asking Arl to come and help. But there wasn't time. Tootie somehow knew Sylvia was in danger—grave danger, and she had to warn her.

The urgency Tootie felt put speed in her feet. She didn't even stop by the palm reading sign to think of what she was going to say. Tootie dashed up to Mrs. Deuce's door and knocked.

There was no answer.

Tootie knocked again.

Still, no answer. Carefully she opened the door and walked inside. Mrs. Deuce and Sylvia were sitting at a round table, not far from the white-painted shelves full of beautiful dolls. Neither had heard her enter. Tootie walked over and stood behind them. Still they did not notice.

Mrs. Deuce was talking in a slow, even manner as she stared in total concentration at the card on the table. "You have suffered through the forces of destiny. Others have controlled your life."

Sylvia also sat staring at the card. Tootie thought she looked as though she were in some sort of trance.

Then Mrs. Deuce turned over another card. It showed a young man suspended upside down by his right ankle from a wooden gallows.

Tootie felt light-headed and there was an undeniable tremor in her limbs. She felt as though a power were reaching out to swallow her. She'd never felt this way in her whole life, and she knew instinctively that this power was evil. It took every bit of her strength, but Tootie reached over between Sylvia and Mrs. Deuce and swept the tarot cards right off the table and onto the floor. Then she grabbed Sylvia by the arm and pulled her to her feet.

"We're leaving!" Tootie announced to the startled expressions of both Sylvia and Mrs. Deuce.

The postmistress's eyes almost bulged out of their sockets. "No one interrupts me when I'm reading!" she said ominously.

"I do!" Tootie announced firmly. She could feel her heart hammering hard against her ribs. "Sylvia is coming with me. She's coming to my house. Now, let's go, Sylvia!"

Sylvia stared openmouthed at Tootie and then back at Mrs. Deuce.

"Move!" Tootie shouted at Sylvia again. "This is no place for you. Come with me."

"W-w-with you?" Sylvia stammered.

"With me," Tootie said with force. "I want you to come to my house. These cards are the devil's cards. You shouldn't be here with them. I've come to help you."

It appeared as though tears came to Sylvia's eyes. Tootie couldn't be sure, but it looked as if Sylvia was about to cry.

Tootie looked at Mrs. Deuce and said with sudden,

unexpected calm, "We're leaving." Then she took Sylvia's arm and pulled her toward the door.

"Come back here!" Mrs. Deuce bellowed. "I'm not finished with you!"

"Run!" Tootie said the moment she and Sylvia were out in the sunlight.

They ran down the country road toward Tootie's farm. Tootie thought she saw Olof going into his parents' barn as they passed, but she and Sylvia kept running.

Finally Tootie spotted the place, toward the back of her parents' forty acres of marshland, where the bus accident had happened. She could see the old Siren bus on its side, still sticking out of the marsh. Suddenly that same feeling, which she had experienced when she realized she was safe after the accident, flooded over her. She knew beyond a doubt that she and Sylvia had escaped something much worse than a bus accident at the Deuces' house.

"Over there!" Tootie shouted and pointed toward the bus. She glanced over her shoulder again to make sure Mrs. Deuce wasn't following them.

Sylvia still hadn't said a word since they had left the postmistress's house. Her black curly hair was bouncing all over her head as she ran, and a few curls began sticking to her flushed, moist face. The sun was beating down on them as they darted for the broken-down bus.

What in the world am I going to say to Sylvia? Tootie thought as she ran. *How am I going to explain?*

All of a sudden it didn't seem to matter. It was as

though she had been set free. The sermon about releasing your enemy from your hatred came to Tootie's mind. It was like a shocking discovery, and the whole thought surprised her.

A big smile spread across Tootie's face as she ran. "We're almost there," she said encouragingly. "Keep going, Sylvia. We'll make it!"

As Tootie and Sylvia neared the old bus, Tootie took the lead and motioned for Sylvia to follow. They bounded around to the other side and finally collapsed on the ground in a heap. Tootie rested for only a second and then scrambled onto her knees and peered around to make sure Mrs. Deuce was nowhere in sight.

"I don't see her," Tootie said. "I don't think she followed us."

Sylvia didn't even try to scan the horizon for Mrs. Deuce. She couldn't. She just remained on the ground, gasping for air. There were so many blotchy red patches on Sylvia's puffy face that it was hard to tell where one blotch started and the next one finished.

"Are you all right?" Tootie asked anxiously, kneeling down beside her.

Sylvia looked up and nodded. Then she said between gasps, "You—came back—for me. Why?"

"I had to," Tootie explained simply. "I prayed, and I just knew I had to help you. That postmistress works for the devil!" Tootie quickly looked around again to make sure they were still alone.

Sylvia's breathing was becoming less frantic, but it was obvious that she was still frightened. "I don't know what happened to me back there," Sylvia admitted. "But I think Mrs. Deuce put some sort of spell on me . . . or tried to hypnotize me . . . or something weird. It was awful!"

Tootie nodded her head in agreement. "It was weird, all right. You didn't even hear me knock. And when I walked in and stood behind you, neither of you even noticed."

Sylvia looked at Tootie with huge eyes. "I couldn't move. I was so scared!"

"We never should've gone into that woman's house in the first place," Tootie announced. "Neither one of us had any business going to a fortune-teller!"

"But I thought she'd help," Sylvia defended in a desperate tone. "I didn't know what else to do! I just had to find out if Mrs. Deuce could make Mama come back home!"

"Your mother?" Tootie asked, totally surprised. "Where is she?"

Sylvia shrugged pathetically.

Tootie realized for the first time that it had been weeks since she'd seen Mrs. Shinler in town. She had figured that Sylvia's mother was on another one of her buying trips and would return soon. Tootie reached out and gently touched Sylvia's hand.

To Tootie's surprise, Sylvia continued to confide in a low whisper, "Mama went to the city to buy some things for the store. But when Daddy called and told her about the robbery and to quit spending money, she screamed at him." Sylvia stopped and took a slow, deep breath. Her eyes reflected a deep hurt as she stared at Tootie. "Mama says she doesn't want to come back," Sylvia admitted slowly. Tears began to roll down her face, and a moan escaped her trembling lips. Finally Sylvia concluded, "Mama says there's nothing left for her anymore here in Siren!"

Tootie could feel tears smarting her eyes. She couldn't imagine a mother not wanting to be with her child—even if that child was Sylvia Shinler. Just as though she were comforting Buddy, Tootie reached over and pulled Sylvia toward her.

Sylvia didn't pull away. Instead, she leaned closer.

"It'll be all right," Tootie said soothingly. "Everything will work out."

Suddenly a horrifying thought crossed Tootie's mind. *What if Sylvia's mother is the bank robber? What if she took the town's money and that's why she won't return?*

As Tootie continued struggling with all these new emotions, Sylvia said, "Your mother loves you, Tootie. I can tell. And I'm sure your father does, too. He sends you letters."

Tootie remembered Sylvia's hurtful comment when Father's letter arrived in Siren. It dawned on her why Sylvia had been so mean and hateful.

Sylvia said in a voice that was barely more than a whisper, "Everyone likes you, Tootie, even Arl."

"He's a good friend," Tootie admitted, remembering Sylvia's conversation with him the night of the pie social when she tried to coax him into bidding on her entry. "But I'm sure Arl wants to be your friend too, Sylvia. Besides, you have loads of friends. There's a whole group of girls who follow you everywhere you go. They're always hanging around you in your parents' store."

Sylvia sat up and looked directly at Tootie. "I give them candy. That's why they're my friends."

Tootie didn't know what to say.

"If my parents lose the store because of this robbery, I don't think those girls will ever come near me again."

"I would," Tootie suddenly admitted.

Sylvia looked at her in surprise. "You would?" she asked with sudden hope in her eyes.

"Sure!" Tootie said and smiled. "After what we've just gone through back there at Mrs. Deuce's, we should be friends for life!"

A huge smile spread across Sylvia's entire face, and the smile totally transformed her appearance. Tootie thought Sylvia looked like a different person when she smiled—almost pretty.

Tootie suddenly giggled. "I can't wait to see the look on everyone's face when they realize we are no longer enemies. It might even disappoint a few people to know we're friends now." She recalled Lavern Roy's comment about wanting to see another fight between her and Sylvia. "I'm sorry for the way I've acted," Tootie admitted. "I never should have pushed you down in the snow that first day we met."

Sylvia's look was mischievous. "If I remember right— I deserved that push."

Tootie jumped up. "Let's make a pact. From here on out, no more fighting!"

"It's a deal!" Sylvia said and shook hands.

Tootie giggled. "Well, friend, why don't you come to my house? Let's see what's for dinner."

As the two began to walk to Tootie's farmhouse, they both noticed how hot and sticky the air had become in the past few minutes. Tootie began telling Sylvia the conversation concerning twisters that she'd heard after church.

Sylvia shrugged. "Every spring the stories get bigger and bigger. It's funny to listen to some of the men, especially Mr. Brightenger. He's always coming up with new tales. I've lived in Siren all of my life and never has a twister come our way. Not once!"

Just then thunder rumbled in the distance. The girls quickly looked to the west and noticed that big black clouds were rolling toward them. They stared at each other in shocked silence and then back at the ominous dark clouds. Thunder rumbled again. Panic spread across both their faces. Neither said a word as they began running toward Tootie's farmhouse. Tootie knew that if it wasn't a twister, it was certainly the most terrible storm that they'd ever seen—and it was coming fast! It was obvious that Sylvia believed the same.

Before they reached the farmyard, Tootie spotted Buddy near the barn. He was trying his best to soothe their cow. But Babe thrashed her head back and forth in a frenzied fashion. Tootie had never seen their big, black-and-white holstein act so strangely.

Then to Tootie's surprise, Babe pulled away from Buddy and started to run. Buddy took off after his cow. And Tootie and Sylvia ran after Buddy.

"Come back, Buddy Boy! Stop!" Tootie yelled. "A storm's coming. You need to get into the house!"

"The cellar!" Sylvia screamed. "We all need to get into the cellar!"

But Buddy kept on running, and so did Babe. She ran straight across the newly plowed garden and headed for a section of the barbed wire fence which Mother had put up just last week.

Tootie, Sylvia, and Buddy were amazed when suddenly Babe leaped to jump the four-foot-high fence. Just as Babe was about to clear the barbed wire, one of her back legs got caught. Blood spurted everywhere. Babe gave a terrible cry, fell momentarily to her knees, then got up and kept running, leaving the barbed wire in a tangled mess.

Buddy screamed after his beloved cow. When he reached the fence, he too looked determined to get over the barrier which now separated him from Babe.

"Stop!" Tootie screamed, as she raced after her brother. She and Sylvia grabbed at his clothes and pulled him back. Buddy fell against them so forcefully that he knocked them over and went down on top.

At that very moment, it began to rain. The downpour pelted their faces, and the sky had turned even darker. By the time Tootie, Sylvia, and Buddy scrambled to their feet, it had started to hail.

"Babe! Babe! Babe!" Buddy wailed.

"Forget her!" Sylvia cried.

"Babe will be all right," Tootie added.

Bright flashes of lightning began to light up the sky. They could hear a strange hissing sound between the crashes of thunder.

Tootie, Sylvia, and Buddy watched in horror as the bottom section of a distant black cloud began to move downward. It formed a long narrow funnel, stretching down from the sky to the ground.

Tootie had never seen anything like it in all of her life. Her knees went weak and freezing fingers of fear spread throughout her thin body. Lightning flashed wildly all about.

"Run!" Tootie suddenly screamed at the top of her lungs. "Run! A twister is coming!"

More lightning flashed, and the smell of sulfur filled the atmosphere as bright streaks zigzagged across the darkened sky. Buddy wiped his nose on his soaked shirtsleeve and shook his head in terror. His almond-shaped eyes were huge as he stared at Tootie and then at Sylvia.

Tootie grabbed Buddy's hand and started to run toward the house. They could all see the black funnel cloud whirling over the back section of the marshland as they ran. The hail continued pelting them and the wind plastered their clothes to their trembling bodies.

Suddenly the wind increased with such fury that it whipped the rain and hail round and round in circles. Then the whirlwind began picking up stones and twigs. The barn doors banged. Tootie, Sylvia, and Buddy kept running with their heads and shoulders bent against the terrible onslaught.

When they finally reached the farmhouse, Mother was standing in the doorway pointing to the black funnel and screaming, "What is that?"

"Quick!" Tootie demanded. "Into the cellar!"

Just then the funnel cloud stretched down so close to the ground that it actually touched. Immediately the hissing noise turned into a loud roar which sounded like a thousand freight trains going by.

"Run!" Tootie and Sylvia screamed and started shoving Buddy and Mother toward the side of the farmhouse where the slanted door to the root cellar leaned against the house. They clung desperately to one another because it felt like the twister was pulling them into its grip. They grasped at the house and then bushes as they struggled against the twister's black tunnel of death.

In his confused panic, Buddy suddenly tried to pull away. Tootie, Sylvia, and Mother had to actually drag Buddy the remaining distance. But when Sylvia and Mother let go to lift the cellar door, Buddy tried to scramble away. Tootie caught his foot. "Inside!" she hollered and shoved Buddy down the two steps after Mother and Sylvia.

Tootie scrambled in on top of them. But before the cellar door slammed shut, Tootie peeked out to get one last look at the twister. To her horror, she saw the tip of the funnel cloud touch the top of the outhouse and pick it up off the ground. She gasped as the cellar door slammed shut and they were left in total darkness.

For the next few terrifying minutes, Tootie, Sylvia, Buddy, and Mother clung to one another in a heap on the cold dirt floor in the pitch-black cellar. It sounded as though the entire farmhouse was being ripped apart over their heads. If any of the others were crying, Tootie couldn't tell because of the deafening sounds from outside. She could feel the pounding of her own heart.

It seemed in those few seconds that her life flashed before her eyes. She could see the faces of Pearl and their father smiling and encouraging them to stay calm. She saw friends from the city and then her new friends from Siren swimming before her eyes—Arl, Lavern, Lawrence, Leo, Mr. Brightenger, and even Pastor Underhill. They were all there as plain as could be in her imagination. A feeling of peace that she'd never experienced before flooded over her. Suddenly the Bible verse that Mother had shared came vividly to her mind.

Tootie quoted out loud, "Peace I leave with you, my peace I give to you; not as the world giveth, give I unto you. Let not your heart be troubled, neither let it be afraid."

Gradually the loud roaring of the twister began to lessen. Tootie wondered if it were heading away from their place toward the Roys' place, or the Olson farm where Arl and his father lived, or the Deuces'. Suddenly she remembered Sylvia and wondered if the Mercantile and the town of Siren would be hit next.

The strange quietness after the storm was almost more frightening than its noise. While they all clung together, Tootie quoted the Bible verse about peace once again.

Eve whispered, "Thanks, lass. I needed to hear that just now." And then Mother sighed deeply. "We're safe. Thank you, God!"

"God! God! God!" Buddy repeated with a quivering voice.

Tootie hugged him more firmly. She knew it would be some time before Buddy would be his old self. He'd seen his beloved cow injure herself trying to scale a barbed wire fence. Then he'd lived through probably the worst twister that had hit Siren, Wisconsin, in all its history. Tootie patted him understandingly and rocked him back and forth in the darkness of the cellar.

"Let's try to sing that song we learned this morning in church," Mother suggested.

Sylvia struggled out of the close circle. "Holey moley!" she screamed. Her voice vibrated back and forth in the cramped space. "I want out of here! I've got to get out of here!"

"Wait," Eve tried to warn. "We need to keep calm. We don't know what we're going to face when we leave this place."

But Sylvia refused to be calmed or comforted. She screamed and thrashed about in the cramped quarters, knocking over the canned goods and supplies which lined the shelves. Buddy began to cry.

"Hold still!" Mother demanded of Sylvia. "There's no room for this."

Tootie inched her way to the door and began to shove upward. It would not budge. "It's stuck!" she cried.

"Don't panic," Eve said.

"Sylvia!" Tootie shouted. "Help me. We've got to push together."

Giving Sylvia something to do seemed to help. She

scooted her way over to the sound of Tootie's voice. Together they shoved their weight against the root cellar door. And with their combined strength, they pushed the door wide open.

But when they looked out, they all gasped. No one could say a word.

Tears smarted Tootie's eyes. A huge lump, which felt as big as a grapefruit, formed in her throat. The barn was practically flattened, its boards and hay strewn all over the place. The water bucket, which they kept inside the barn door for washing hands, was now in the front yard and dented almost beyond recognition. The barbed wire fence was twisted into a crude giant bundle. And most shocking of all, the tamarack tree had been uprooted and lay on its side with its huge roots exposed and dangling. And, of course, the outhouse was totally gone, as was Babe.

"What are we going to do?" Tootie asked in a woeful whisper.

Eve quickly reminded her, "We've got insurance on the place. Besides, we're safe. That's what matters the most."

"Babe! Babe! Babe!" Buddy cried.

Suddenly Sylvia began to scream. She shoved Tootie, Buddy, and Eve aside and scrambled the rest of the way out of the cellar. She ran around the McCarthys' farmyard in a frenzy. Then she began circling the uprooted tamarack tree.

"Leave her be," Mother suggested as she stepped out of the cellar with Tootie and Buddy close behind. "I don't think anything will calm that girl. She'll exhaust herself soon enough."

The three stood together and stared at their house. It had been twisted more than an inch or two off its foundation. The screen door was gone and all the windows had been ripped out. Also, part of the roof had been peeled back. It had stopped raining, but the rain from the storm had obviously done a lot of damage to their home.

"Everything's ruined!" Tootie exclaimed, failing to keep the panic out of her voice.

"We need to be thankful," Mother reminded her again. "It would have been much worse if you and Sylvia hadn't shoved us into the root cellar. All this can be repaired." Eve spread her hands. "That was quick thinking, lass."

"Babe! Babe! Babe!" Buddy continued to whimper.

Tootie took her little brother into her arms and let him cry out his misery.

Just then the Roys arrived in their truck. Mr. and Mrs. Roy hurried out of the front, while the three boys jumped off the back.

"You're safe!" Lawrence shouted with great relief as he reached Tootie's side.

"Yes," Tootie said. "We're safe and sound, but look at this place!"

The Roys stared around at the total mess of the McCarthy farm. They looked at the flattened barn, the twisted house, and then stared in disbelief at Sylvia running around the uprooted tree.

Lavern asked, "Did the twister pick her up in town and drop her out here?"

Tootie almost wanted to laugh at the shocked expressions on the Roys' faces. Even Mr. and Mrs. Roy looked as though they had been thinking the same thing.

"No," Tootie admitted. "Sylvia was here for dinner. She helped me get Mother and Buddy into the cellar just in time."

"My daughter and that Shinler girl did some mighty quick thinking," Eve admitted. "They practically had to drag Buddy and me to the cellar. I was so scared I could hardly move. That storm came in fast!"

"It was fast and furious," Mrs. Roy agreed.

Mr. Roy added, "We saw the twister moving straight toward your place. We wanted to come and warn you, but there wasn't time."

Lavern interrupted, "We didn't know if we were going to find you dead or alive!"

"We're alive!" Tootie shouted, opening wide her arms, and twirled in a circle.

"Alive! Alive! Alive!" Buddy repeated, clapping his hands.

"We've got to get going," Mr. Roy interjected quickly. "We need to check on the rest of the neighbors and then head into town to make sure everyone is safe."

"We're coming with you," Eve announced. "We might be needed."

Tootie felt proud of her mother.

"But look at your place," Mrs. Roy said. "Don't you want to—"

"No," Eve said. "This can wait. Let's go!"

Everyone hurried over to the truck except for Tootie. She darted after Sylvia and grabbed her arm. "Come on, Sylvia," Tootie demanded. "Come with us!"

Tootie and Sylvia piled into the back of the truck next to Buddy and the Roy boys. While Mr. Roy pulled away from what was left of the McCarthy farm, Tootie stared out at her home. The lump in her throat seemed to get bigger and bigger as she realized how truly fortunate they were to have survived the terrible twister.

The narrow country road was strewn with branches that had been ripped off trees. There were also large sections of roofing lying here and there on the road. Tootie recognized some of it as coming from their own house. Suddenly Mr. Roy stepped on his brakes. Then he slowly maneuvered the truck around a wringer washing machine. It was sitting upright and undamaged on one side of the road. Tootie wondered whose it was.

When they finally got to the Olsons' farm, they saw the barn was still standing, but there was a lot of damage. Part of the roof and one entire side were gone. They could see Arl and Olof Olson chasing a half dozen crazed cows, trying to corral them into what was left of the barn.

Mr. Roy stopped the truck and he, his wife, and Tootie's mother hurried over to where the Olsons and Arl's dad stood near the farmhouse door looking inside at the damage.

Tootie, Buddy, Lavern, Lawrence, and Leo jumped out of the back of the truck and ran to join Arl and Olof. Buddy was crying, "Olof! Olof! Olof!"

Arl smiled broadly at Tootie and Buddy and then at the Roys. "I'm glad you're all safe!" he said.

"And you, too," Tootie said, feeling truly grateful.

Nobody had noticed Sylvia. She remained in the back of the truck all by herself. Finally she stood up and screamed, "I can't stay here, you stupid people! I've got to get home!" Sylvia jumped out of the truck and started running down the road toward town.

"Don't mind her," Tootie defended her new friend. "If Sylvia and I haven't reached town by the time you do, pick us up on the way." Then to everyone's surprise, Tootie tore off after Sylvia.

"Stop!" Tootie hollered.

But Sylvia kept running.

"Stop!" Tootie hollered again.

Sylvia slowed her pace. Her eyes were huge as she looked at Tootie. "Do you think Mama will come home when she hears about this twister? Do you think she'll come and see if Daddy and I are safe?"

"Sure," Tootie said, trying her best to encourage her new friend. But once again Tootie wondered if Mrs. Shinler were the bank robber and if anyone would ever see her again.

They were approaching the palm reading sign in front of Mrs. Deuce's house when suddenly Tootie and Sylvia stopped and stared in disbelief. It looked as though the postmistress's entire house had come apart at the seams. Tootie couldn't believe she and Sylvia had been in that house only hours earlier.

"Do you think she's dead?" Sylvia whispered.

Just then they spotted Mrs. Deuce walking around on the far side where the fireplace used to stand. She was calling over and over, "My crystal ball—my cards—my crystal ball—my cards."

Then Tootie and Sylvia noticed Julius near what remained of the woodpile. He was frantically throwing wood into a heap, piece by piece. Tootie wondered why he cared about the pile of chopped wood at a time like this.

"Forget about that crystal ball of yours!" Julius demanded of his mother. "It didn't help you to predict this storm, so good riddance to it and those tarot cards!"

It was then that Julius looked across the street and noticed Tootie and Sylvia. He glared at them and hollered, "What are you two staring at? Get out of here!"

Tootie was convinced that both Mrs. Deuce and her son had gone completely mad.

Mrs. Deuce looked their way. She started walking toward them through the litter. Her eyes were wild and her hair was standing on end.

Tootie wanted to run.

Mrs. Deuce hollered, "All my son cares about are his precious dolls!"

"Shut up!" Julius shouted.

But her son couldn't stop her. Mrs. Deuce kept right on talking. "Before the storm hit, do you know what my son was doing?"

Tootie and Sylvia stared openmouthed at the woman who was still marching toward them. "No," Tootie said bravely, "we have no idea what Julius was up to."

"Shut up, Ma!" Julius hollered again.

"My son dashed around stuffing all his precious dolls into a gunnysack," Mrs. Deuce continued. "Can you imagine? He was more concerned about his dolls than he was about me. He saved them all—all except for one!" She turned and glared maliciously at her enraged son. "The twister hit before you saved that last doll, didn't it?" Then the postmistress threw back her head and laughed wickedly.

Tootie and Sylvia didn't want to stand there a minute longer and hear the two argue over some foolish doll collection. Tootie said, "I'm glad you're safe, Mrs. Deuce. We're going into town to check on Sylvia's father."

"That's right," Sylvia quickly added.

Then they both turned and ran. But after they'd gone about one hundred yards, Tootie noticed something odd off the road on the left-hand side. She stopped for a second and stared. Instinctively she knew what it was.

Sylvia glanced her way.

"Keep going," Tootie said. "I want to check on something. I'll catch up with you in a few minutes."

Sylvia nodded and ran ahead.

Tootie looked at the little doll that was sticking head first into the side of a tree. She had recognized it immediately because of the bright red-and-yellow dress. It was the same doll she had admired that afternoon at Mrs. Deuce's. It would only take a second to rescue the little thing and then she'd join Sylvia. Tootie walked quickly toward the doll, not suspecting the shocking discovery she was about to make.

The force of the twister had somehow shoved the doll's porcelain head directly into the bark of the tree, leaving the cloth body in its surrounding bright colorful dress, sticking straight out. It looked almost like a red-and-yellow flower attached to the side of the tree. All the stories about the odd things that twisters do flashed through Tootie's mind.

Tootie knew she was far enough away from the Deuces' house that they couldn't see her, but she still looked around just in case Julius or his mother had followed. They had both reacted so strangely over the loss of this doll that Tootie wasn't about to draw attention to it. She decided she would wait until they both calmed down and then she would return the little thing.

With great care, Tootie began to pull on the neatly stitched cloth body to see if she could remove the doll from the tree without damaging it. Immediately the porcelain head shattered into dozens of pieces and the headless doll fell from the tree and landed at her feet. When she leaned over to pick it up, she discovered that the cloth body was stuffed with money! Rolls of tens, twenties, fifties, and hundred-dollar bills filled the arms and legs of the little doll!

What is Julius Deuce doing with all this money? But the moment she asked the question, she knew. *He's the robber!*

Tootie looked around again, her heart racing. Quickly she gathered every piece of the broken porcelain head and piled them together at the base of the tree. *This is evidence,* she thought. *Where should I put it?*

She began stuffing everything into the pockets of her navy serge dress—the same one she'd worn to church that morning. The dress had two big pockets on the skirt. The broken doll's head with the little limp body went into one pocket, and the rolls of stolen money into the other. Tootie looked down to make sure none of the material of the red-and-yellow lace dress was sticking out. The lace wasn't showing, but both pockets bulged out in front. She knew if anyone saw her, they'd ask what she was carrying.

For a few moments, Tootie practiced walking back and forth in a casual manner. Then she hurried to the road and looked around. Sylvia was far away and Tootie didn't want to draw attention to herself by calling to her. And she certainly didn't want to head back in the direction they had just come past the Deuces' place. *If they see me,* Tootie thought, *I don't know what I will do!*

"I've got to get this to the sheriff," she said out loud, knowing she had to stay calm and think clearly. "Oh, God, help me!"

Tootie started walking toward town. All the while she tried to think of the best way to expose Julius Deuce. She realized she couldn't prove the money in the doll was the stolen bank money, but she knew beyond a doubt that it was.

Suddenly she saw visions of Julius throwing wood into the pile beside their ruined house. She recalled the words of Mrs. Deuce about how her son had run around before the twister hit, stuffing his precious doll collection into a gunnysack. *I bet there is money inside every one of those dolls,* Tootie thought. *And the whole lot of them are out there in a gunnysack under that pile of wood. All of them—except for one!* Tootie patted her bulging pockets and kept walking, more determined than ever.

Excitement replaced fear as she whispered to herself, "I've solved the mystery. I'm going to get that reward money! Two hundred and fifty-two dollars!"

In her mind she could see Father and Pearl returning home. Tootie thought that they might even have enough reward money to buy that abandoned bakery in town and set up a pie business. She could see her father standing proudly behind the shiny counter in his three-piece suit and handsome smile. Pearl would be standing beside him. Then Tootie thought of using some of her reward money to get Pearl's teeth fixed. *That will bring Pearl home for sure!* Tootie took several deep breaths to calm her racing heart.

Just then Mr. Roy drove up behind her and honked his horn. Tootie jumped so high she thought the evidence would fly right out of her pockets.

"Climb on!" the Roy boys hollered from the back of the truck.

"Hurry, Tootie," her mother added from the front seat. "We want to check on everyone in town."

"Toot! Toot! Toot!" Buddy cried.

"I thought you were with Sylvia," Lavern Roy said.

"She's up ahead," Tootie explained as calmly as she could.

It was not going to be easy getting into the back of the truck with her pockets stuffed full. Just then Arl Neilson reached out his hand.

"Thanks!" Tootie said and grabbed his hand so he could pull her up into the back of the truck. She quickly sat down between Arl and Buddy.

"Oh, goodness me!" Lavern teased. "We have a gentleman in our midst." Lavern jabbed Arl in the side.

Tootie ignored Lavern's comment, made sure the stuffing in her pockets was hidden, and then quickly put her arm around Buddy so he could lean his head against her.

As the truck proceeded toward town, Arl explained, "Everything's all right back at the Olsons'. We got those cows calmed down, and my dad and Mr. Olson are putting tarps over the bare spots in the roof of the house."

"But when we offered to help the Deuces," Lawrence interrupted, "they wanted nothing to do with us. Mrs. Deuce walked around like a crazy woman looking for her crystal ball."

"And Julius Deuce demanded that we leave!" Leo added.

Tootie knew why, but she decided to keep her discovery a secret until she had contacted Sheriff Collins.

Soon they stopped and picked up Sylvia and took her the rest of the way into town. Tootie wanted to tell Sylvia that her mother wasn't the bank robber. But she knew Sylvia had never once suspected her own mother of the crime. Tootie determined that she would never let Sylvia know what she had thought. She reached out and squeezed Sylvia's hand. They smiled at each other with understanding.

The Roy boys and Arl exchanged glances. But no one said a word.

To everyone's surprise, the twister had missed the town of Siren altogether. The strong winds had done some minor damage, but not one building had been destroyed. Mr. Brightenger had gathered together a group of men and women and they were eager to go out to the countryside and help every farmer who had been in the pathway of the twister. Pastor Underhill had joined the circle of willing helpers. Even Mr. Shinler was among the crowd.

"Daddy!" Sylvia cried the moment she saw him. She jumped out of the back of the truck and ran to his side. "Has Mama come?"

"No," Mr. Shinler said. "But where have you been? I was worried to death about you!"

"Sylvia was with us," Tootie answered. She had remained in the truck next to Buddy.

Mr. Brightenger's expression was filled with concern as he looked at Tootie and then at her mother and the Roy family. "Some of us here in town saw that twister forming in the distance. It looked like it was heading straight for the farms in your area."

"It was," Mr. Roy replied. "But the McCarthys' place was hit harder than ours. The Olsons have a lot of damage, and the Deuces' place is beyond repair."

Mr. Shinler stepped forward with his daughter at his side. "At times like this, we need to help one another. I'm sure my store has all the supplies you will need."

"Thank you," Eve said with a big smile. "But you'll be paid for everything, Mr. Shinler. I have insurance on the farm."

"Twister insurance?" Mr. Brightenger asked in great surprise. "Now that's being prepared!"

Everyone laughed.

It was four o'clock in the afternoon by the time the townsfolk were ready with all the supplies. They planned to follow Mr. Roy and help each of the twister victims along the way. The trucks were full of food, containers of water, tarpaulins, dry firewood, and some emergency building supplies. They were going to help set up shelters for the night. Tootie didn't know all the exact plans because she had remained in the back of Mr. Roy's truck huddled close to her brother. No one thought anything about Tootie's lack of involvement because Buddy needed comforting. He kept crying, "Babe! Babe! Babe!"

"Are you sure Sheriff Collins isn't here?" Tootie asked Sylvia for the second time.

"I'm sure," Sylvia responded. "Daddy says he went to Webster for the weekend. Why?"

"I'll tell you later," Tootie confided. "I hope your mother comes back soon."

Sylvia's look was strained. "Me, too. And I hope your dad and sister move back to Siren, honest I do."

Tootie smiled. "We're going to be best of friends, Sylvia Shinler. I just know it!" Then suddenly a new thought dawned on her. "Hey, would you come back to my place? I need your help with something!"

"Sure," Sylvia responded quickly. "I know Daddy won't mind."

The sky had finally cleared, and the sun began to shine as Mr. Roy and the small caravan of helpers left town. Sylvia sat on the other side of Buddy and tried to help comfort him. The Roy boys and Arl were holding onto the supplies as they bounced over the rough roads.

They stopped to deliver a few things at the Deuces', but neither Mrs. Deuce nor Julius welcomed them. Tootie stared at the pile of wood; her heart raced faster. "I know what you're hiding under there," she felt like yelling for all to hear. But she knew that now was not the time—she had to keep her secret a little longer.

Arl jumped off at the Olsons' place and helped unload what was needed there. Then he came back to the truck. "My dad and I will be over tomorrow, Tootie. We'll do what we can to help."

"Thanks," Tootie said and smiled. "See you tomorrow."

"Good-bye," Arl yelled and waved as the truck pulled away. "Good-bye, Sylvia," he added.

Sylvia waved back excitedly. The Roy boys looked at each other and raised their eyebrows.

The moment Mr. Roy stopped in front of the McCarthy farm by the uprooted tamarack, Mother hurried to Tootie's side. "It's going to upset Buddy to be around here for the next few minutes. There's still plenty of daylight left. So why don't you take him for a walk and try to keep him calm."

This fit perfectly with Tootie's idea. She had wanted somehow to get out to the old school bus and hide the valuable evidence inside one of the seats. With all the people around their place doing repairs, Tootie knew the doll and money wouldn't be safe anywhere else.

Tootie and Sylvia each took one of Buddy's hands and led him out toward the back forty acres of marshland. The ground was still firm after the long winter months. They could see the wreckage lying on its side, and Tootie felt thankful it had not been disturbed by the twister.

As they approached the front of the bus, they heard a cry. Tootie felt certain it was Julius Deuce. *He's discovered that I have his doll! He's after me!* Tootie thought. She broke out in a cold sweat.

Just then the cry came again. This time it sounded more like a wounded animal. And out from behind the bus walked Babe. The wound on her back leg had stopped bleeding and she limped slightly, but otherwise Babe looked fine. She mooed contentedly.

"Babe! Babe! Babe!" Buddy cried and rushed to her side. He nestled his cheek against Babe's soft muzzle and sobbed. The joy of watching her brother's excitement at seeing his beloved cow almost made Tootie forget what she needed to do.

"Watch him," Tootie whispered to Sylvia. "I'll be right back." Tootie walked around to the other side of the wreckage and carefully climbed inside. She knew the backseat was loose because it had come completely off during the accident. Very cautiously she removed the evidence from her pockets and hid it under the seat—the dozens of pieces of painted porcelain, the limp body of the cloth doll, and finally the rolls of money. Then she darted back to Sylvia and Buddy.

On their walk back to the farm, while Buddy was patting and mumbling endearments to his cow, Tootie told Sylvia what she had discovered.

"You're kidding!" Sylvia exclaimed. "The money was inside those pretty dolls? I can't believe it. It was in plain view all the time! I looked right at those dolls!"

"And I know where the rest of the money is hidden," Tootie confided. She told Sylvia about the woodpile. "But I have to get all this information to Sheriff Collins. And somehow it has to be proved that the money in the dolls is really the stolen money."

"Don't worry," Sylvia said. "I'm sure there are ways to prove that. Sheriff Collins will probably come tomorrow. I heard that the people of Webster were going to be notified of our disaster and that they would send over some workers."

Tootie sighed deeply. "Good!"

Suddenly a radiant smile spread across Sylvia's face.

"This means that all our money will be returned to the bank! Maybe Mama will come home!"

"And I get the reward money!" Tootie added.

That night Mother, Buddy, Sylvia, and Tootie settled down to sleep in a corner of the kitchen. The folks from town had piled mattresses and blankets on the floor and made it as comfortable as possible. A fire had been built in the woodstove, and boards had been nailed to openings where the windows used to be. Several families had invited Eve to move in temporarily with them, but she wanted to stay in her own farmhouse. They had enough food and water to last for a couple of days. Everyone had promised to come back and start some of the repairs in the morning.

Tootie thought she would have a hard time falling to sleep crowded together on the two dry mattresses in the corner of the kitchen, but exhaustion won out. Before she knew it, she was sound asleep.

In the morning when the truckloads of people arrived, Sheriff Collins was with them. He and a number of Webster folks had come ready to work. The Roys were there, as were Arl and Mr. Neilson.

"Before the work begins," Tootie announced loudly, "I want you all to follow me. I want to show you something."

"What's going on, Tootie?" Mother asked.

"Please, this is really important," Tootie pleaded. "I've solved the bank robbery!"

A gasp could be heard around the crowd. Sheriff

Collins stepped forward. "I have a suspect in mind," he said. "But I can't prove a thing."

"I can!" Tootie said.

With great excitement, the entire crowd followed Tootie and Sylvia out behind the McCarthy farm. Buddy walked beside Tootie, while Arl and the Roy boys hurried to catch up. As the crowd neared the old wreckage, Tootie ran ahead and climbed into the bus to the surprise of everyone. When she emerged, she held up the headless doll in one hand and the money in the other.

"I found this money!" she announced. "It was hidden inside this doll."

Sheriff Collins moved to Tootie's side. "I recognize that doll. It comes from Julius Deuce's collection. I saw it when I questioned him."

"That's right," Tootie admitted. "The twister picked this doll up, and I found it stuck headfirst into the side of a tree."

"Julius Deuce is my number one suspect," Sheriff Collins admitted. "In fact, the only thing missing was proof. And I believe, young lady, that you have just supplied the evidence we need."

Mumbling could be heard from a number of the town council members.

Sheriff Collins held up his hands. "All right, everybody, don't get all riled. I will arrest Julius. But he is still innocent until proven guilty." Then he added, "However, it looks like this will be a simple matter for the court to decide, especially after all the other information I have discovered about the man. We will need to identify this as the stolen money," Sheriff Collins concluded, "and find where he has hidden the rest."

"I know where it is!" Tootie announced.

"But don't say it out loud," Sheriff Collins warned. "We'll continue this conversation in private." Then the sheriff began to laugh. "You have left very little for me to do, Miss Tootie McCarthy. It appears you've solved this case all by yourself. And, if all goes as planned, you will be receiving the reward money."

"Hurray!" Sylvia shouted.

"Hurray!" Arl, the Roy boys, Buddy, Mother, and several others added.

Tootie looked around at the crowd in front of her. She didn't know what the future would hold. She didn't know if Father or Pearl would really come back home, or if they would get that bakery in town as she hoped. But no matter what—Tootie somehow knew in her heart that she would have the strength to face each challenge.

Mother stepped over and put her arm around Tootie. She whispered into her ear, "I am singing it with you, lass."

"Singing what?" Tootie asked.

"It is well, it is well with my soul!"

"That's it!" Tootie said. "That's exactly how I'm feeling!" She smiled at her mother and then at her friends. "Come on!" Tootie said. "What are we waiting for? We have work to do!"